Art Fiction

Stories

Art Fiction

Stories

Edited by Genevieve Sheets

PP

Portmay Press
New York

"Wade's Technique" was originally published in *All Most*.

All images courtesy of the Metropolitan Museum of Art's Open Access initiative

Cover image: Fitz Henry Lane (formerly Fitz Hugh Lane), *Stage Fort Across Gloucester Harbor*, 1862, The Metropolitan Museum of Art, New York, Purchase, Rogers and Fletcher Funds, Erving and Joyce Wolf Fund, Raymond J. Horowitz Gift, Bequest of Richard De Wolfe Brixey, by exchange, and John Osgood and Elizabeth Amis Cameron Blanchard Memorial Fund, 1978

Project management and design by Emily Albarillo
Printed in the United States of America
First published in 2019 by Portmay Press, New York
This paperback edition published in 2019 by Portmay Press, New York
Library of Congress Control Number: 2019941575

ISBN 978-0-9994006-9-2 (pb)

PUBLISHER'S CATALOGING-IN-PUBLICATION DATA
(Prepared by The Donohue Group, Inc.)

Names: Sheets, Genevieve, editor. | Container of (work): Chopin, Kate, 1850-1904. Point at issue! | Container of (work): D'Agincourt, Maryann. Wade's technique. | Container of (work): Wharton, Edith, 1862-1937. Portrait. | Container of (work): James, Henry, 1843-1916. Landscape painter. | Container of (work): Cather, Willa, 1873-1947. Wagner matinee.
Title: Art fiction stories / edited by Genevieve Sheets.
Description: New York : Portmay Press, [2019] | Summary: "Each story has been paired with a work of art from the Metropolitan Museum of Art. In the following introduction, Genevieve Sheets explores themes found throughout the collection and explains her motivations in choosing the pieces of art to accompany the stories"--Introduction.
Identifiers: ISBN 9780999400647 (hardcover) | ISBN 9780999400654 (ebook)
Subjects: LCSH: Arts in literature. | Artists--Fiction. | Musicians--Fiction. | LCGFT: Short stories.
Classification: LCC PS509.A76 A78 2019 (print) | LCC PS509.A76 (ebook) | DDC 810.80357--dc23

PP
Portmay Press
244 Madison Avenue
New York, NY 10016
www.portmaypress.com

Art Fiction

Stories

Edited by Genevieve Sheets

PP

Portmay Press
New York

All images courtesy of the Metropolitan Museum of Art's Open Access initiative

Cover image: Fitz Henry Lane (formerly Fitz Hugh Lane), *Stage Fort Across Gloucester Harbor*, 1862, The Metropolitan Museum of Art, New York, Purchase, Rogers and Fletcher Funds, Erving and Joyce Wolf Fund, Raymond J. Horowitz Gift, Bequest of Richard De Wolfe Brixey, by exchange, and John Osgood and Elizabeth Amis Cameron Blanchard Memorial Fund, 1978

Project management and design by Emily Albarillo
Printed in the United States of America
First published in 2019 by Portmay Press, New York
This paperback edition published in 2019 by Portmay Press, New York
Library of Congress Control Number: 2019941575

ISBN 978-0-9994006-9-2 (pb)

PUBLISHER'S CATALOGING-IN-PUBLICATION DATA
(Prepared by The Donohue Group, Inc.)

Names: Sheets, Genevieve, editor. | Container of (work): Chopin, Kate, 1850-1904. Point at issue! | Container of (work): D'Agincourt, Maryann. Wade's technique. | Container of (work): Wharton, Edith, 1862-1937. Portrait. | Container of (work): James, Henry, 1843-1916. Landscape painter. | Container of (work): Cather, Willa, 1873-1947. Wagner matinee.
Title: Art fiction stories / edited by Genevieve Sheets.
Description: New York : Portmay Press, [2019] | Summary: "Each story has been paired with a work of art from the Metropolitan Museum of Art. In the following introduction, Genevieve Sheets explores themes found throughout the collection and explains her motivations in choosing the pieces of art to accompany the stories"--Introduction.
Identifiers: ISBN 9780999400647 (hardcover) | ISBN 9780999400654 (ebook)
Subjects: LCSH: Arts in literature. | Artists--Fiction. | Musicians--Fiction. | LCGFT: Short stories.
Classification: LCC PS509.A76 A78 2019 (print) | LCC PS509.A76 (ebook) | DDC 810.80357--dc23

PP
Portmay Press
244 Madison Avenue
New York, NY 10016
www.portmaypress.com

Introduction

Art Fiction: Stories *is the first in an innovative series of collected works of art fiction. Each story in this volume was chosen for the unique way in which the author "paints with words" and, whether from the perspective of the nineteenth century, the twentieth, or the twenty-first, embraces the intersections of art, life, and fiction. Each story has been paired with a work of art from the Metropolitan Museum of Art. In the following introduction, Genevieve Sheets explores themes found throughout the collection and explains her motivations in choosing the pieces of art to accompany the stories.*

A common belief is that those in the "artistic class," usually designated as such by education and/or wealth, have the most refined tastes. I think these stories belie that conclusion quite well. Most of the works in this collection also have a sly feminist slant, almost a twist. Only one of the stories was written by a man, Henry James. Yet he was not necessarily a typical male author of his time. The man/woman relationship is a theme that links the stories, generally in a unique or untraditional context.

A Point at Issue!

Kate Chopin, 1889

Eleanor and Charles Faraday, the couple who are the subject of "A Point at Issue!," have a fairly untraditional marriage, from her reluctance to thrust the announcement of the wedding into the public eye to their decision to always be open and honest with each other and maintain their individual natures. At a time when independence after marriage is usually expected for men, Charles considering Eleanor as his equal in intellect and wanting her to maintain her individuality is groundbreaking.

When Eleanor follows up their quiet nuptials with the decision to stay alone in Paris for the academic year to fully immerse herself in the language—with her husband's blessing, no less—the other residents of their college town of Plymdale are in shock.

Eleanor and Charles are early feminists, and she can probably be called an introvert as well. While she is independent in her thoughts and actions, her emotional attachment to Charles, and her subsequent jealousy of his admiration for another woman, is understandable—her reactive letter puzzles the ignorant Charles, but the "deluge" of ardent letters that follow assures him of Eleanor's passion for him, and he thinks no more of the issue (at least temporarily).

While the story repeatedly points out Eleanor and Charles's independent relationship, Charles seems less aware of his own conservatism as he easily reverts back to bachelorhood "as quietly as though it had been interrupted but by the interval of a day." Although Charles spends time with the Beacons (an ideal traditional family), he objects to his wife's meetings with a handsome and mysterious Frenchman, and is inspired to paint the street red with the other man's "villainous blood." And of course, the final two lines of the story underline this hypocrisy.

I have selected *The Letter* by Camille Corot, circa 1865, to accompany this story. I can picture the melancholic wife in her nondescript Parisian flat, reading the letter that devastates her. I like how well this painting reflects the essence of the story. The forlorn woman holding a letter is a nice depiction of the scene in which Eleanor reads of her new husband's careless admission of admiration for the young Kitty. I think it appropriate as it brings to mind a moment of Eleanor's time alone in Paris.

Wade's Technique

Maryann D'Agincourt, 2013

D'Agincourt's work is full of imagery and light; her stream-of-consciousness writing is reminiscent of Virginia Woolf and Henry James, and her descriptions are evocative. Her characters almost always have a deep appreciation of art, and their stories center on how this affects their lives both negatively and positively.

Gregory is the main focus of "Wade's Technique," and he examines himself in the context of two lovers at very different times in his life. As a young man of twenty, Gregory meets a German photographer, Karin, while traveling on his own in Europe, and they have a short but intense relationship. Karin's frankness takes Gregory aback, and he feels more exposed than usual. During a particularly uncomfortable conversation, he admits to her that his detached nature keeps him from having depth or forming meaningful relationships, but soon after, he decides that he will not contact Karin again once they part. For he has revealed to her, "I do not want to be who I am," explaining that his passivity has always been an issue. But after a week of being alone again, Gregory has the urge to contact her. He has made this impossible by discarding her phone number, and he is unable to reach her through other means.

And in the present day, at age thirty-five, he finds himself in a similar place when analyzing his relationship with Sheila, an artist, who teaches at the same school as Gregory. Their romance is irregular; sometimes passionate; often intellectual. But he admits "that he had been seeing Sheila for a little over two years, and he frankly did not know her." The reader might wonder if that is by design, so he can maintain some closeness without needing to back away, as he needs to do in Germany. And it must not be coincidence that Sheila's stride is balletic, which reminds him of Karin, another graceful walker. It strikes him that he's been seeing Sheila for two years and doesn't really know her, but he opens up to Karin within two and a half weeks.

When the couple discuss Adam Wade, an artist Sheila admires, Gregory finds his work "desolate" and "bland," while Sheila is inspired by his simplicity. Gregory describes himself as a realist—is this related? Is that why he doesn't connect with people? Or has that changed, fifteen years after Karin? In Germany, "[Gregory] was moving through life, detached and alone." He forces himself to discontinue his intimacy with Karin. Has that changed with Sheila? Is Sheila the "temporary replacement" in his life as well as in her profession as a substitute art teacher?

At one point, Sheila tells Gregory that when she was young her father died and ever since then art has become her focus and her constant. She is able to see movement in art, in a way that seems impossible but fascinating, and has escaped to art museums to experience life in the paintings. Her career is art; her life is art. Gregory thinks, "Yet Sheila—she had had such a harsh background, and had transcended her past. Hadn't she?" Or is her immersion in art merely a response to the sadness in her home following her father's death?

I know a Degas will be appropriate to accompany this story as soon as the author describes Karin's balletic walk, even before Sheila and Gregory visit the museum where they view a Degas painting. Although many of Degas's ballerinas are in repose, or warming up, or preparing for rehearsal or performance, I have chosen *Dancer Onstage*, circa 1877, because it feels to me like we are watching the dancer in the middle of a movement or performance, as we are contemplating the protagonists in the midst of their respective lives.

The Portrait

Edith Wharton, 1899

According to the partygoers in the prologue to the story, art is only admired if it shows the sitter as pretty and ideal, but Mrs. Mellish, the hostess, explains that a true artist doesn't have those blinders and sees many sides to his sitters. A true artist knows that this is what makes a real person. A party-goer who is described only as a "pretty woman" proves this point by exclaiming that a "sumptuously empty" portrait by Lillo, the protagonist, is the "only nice picture he ever did." She clearly will not approve of her likeness being painted in any way but ideal!

Does Vard kill himself because in reality he is not the confident, dazzling, charismatic figure he has been assumed to be? And because Lillo's painting reflects that? Lillo says of his own painting that "when one tries to fail one can make such a complete success of it." Later he says, "It certainly is a complete disguise," as he looks at the portrait. But does he mean the likeness of Vard, or Vard himself?

The narrator sees the quick crayon sketch of Vard's daughter as "genius," while remembering the actual person as "showy yet ineffective"; "seen without seeing"—her portrait belies the narrator's memory of her personality. And when Lillo reveals the narrator's blindness to her true nature, the narrator takes "comfort to think that fate had made [Vard] expiate our weakness." Is Vard's suicide a sacrificial redemption of the sins of the narrator and his friends? Vard is clearly no savior and no unblemished lamb.

Lillo perceives Vard, when they first meet, as magnificent and scandalous. That changes when Lillo starts to get to know him through his daughter, and when he starts sitting for Lillo: "His depth was a false perspective painted on a wall." How can Lillo paint the depth and interest of a man who turns out to have none? Not only is the magnificence illusory, Vard isn't even evil enough to be scandalous: "morally he wasn't bad enough; his corruption wasn't sufficiently imaginative to be interesting." If Lillo is true to his own genius, he will reveal this mediocrity in his masterpiece. Instead, because he finds Miss Vard so adorable, and doesn't want to disappoint her with the reality of her father, he sets out to fail.

Despite Lillo's adoration for this woman, and how much he gives up for her, he never sees her as his equal. His chauvinism is evident from the beginning of the story, in his reference to "fellows who know," when it's obvious that Mrs. Mellish knows more about art than anyone else we've met. At the end, he tosses off the opinion that "you can make a woman [in this case, Miss Vard] believe almost anything she doesn't quite understand."

The caricature *The Art Connoisseurs*, drawn by Louis Léopold Boilly in 1823–28, fits perfectly with my mental image of the art critics in the first scene of this story: examining the work closely and in a crowd without really seeing its beauty and meaning. This drawing is so evocative of that first scene of "art critics," quotations strongly stressed, who chatter away about how much they know about artwork when, in fact, they remain largely ignorant of it.

A Landscape Painter

Henry James, 1866

The central plot of this story revolves around Locksley, a wealthy yet heartbroken man who wants to take a break from his life as a rich society gentleman and escape to rural

New England. This decision is almost certainly predicated by his broken engagement, to a woman who has revealed she was only after Locksley for his fortune. He hopes that being away from that kind of life will allow him to believe that there is more to himself than his wealth: "I have determined to stand upon my own merits. If they fail me, I shall fall back upon my millions; but with God's help I will test them, and see what kind of stuff I am made of."

When he arrives at his destination, and soon after meets the old sailor Captain Blunt, he declares, "bless his simple heart!" even as he gives his impression that the old sailor speaks as though Locksley is the fortunate one to be associating with him. Wealth seems to be the only thing that gives a man the right to this attitude, in Locksley's opinion.

The Captain isn't the only person Locksley dismisses straightaway only to be proven wrong later in the story. Before he meets Captain Blunt's daughter, he regards her as a "dark spot": "I suppose she's over thirty. I think I know the species." In speaking of the household in general: "[Captain Blunt's] needs and habits are of the simplest kind. What does he or his daughter know of the great worldly theory of necessities, the great worldly scale of pleasures?" So, in Locksley's opinion, can the poor not appreciate beauty and art? It certainly doesn't seem so. But it's not long before Locksley's dismissal of Miss Blunt turns to admiration: she is "emphatically the portrait of a lady." Can the narrator's point of view be changing in this new environment? In fact, he begins to appreciate her simple style and life as a working woman: "This working-day side of her character is what especially pleases me in Miss Blunt. This holy working-dress of loveliness and dignity sits upon her with the simplicity of an antique drapery. Little use has she for whalebones and furbelows. What a poetry there is, after all, in red hands!"

Although Locksley's journey takes him from a judgmental member of upper-class society to one who loves and accepts joyfully into his life "simpler" things and people, the tragedy of the story is that nothing changes in the end, and he is still treated differently because of his fortune. Is his foray, his immersion into art and painting utterly fruitless? Or, when he dies a few years later, does he have a little more understanding of the simple life?

For this story I have chosen *Stage Fort Across Gloucester Harbor*, painted by Fitz Henry Lane in 1862. The magnificence of the sky reminds me of the work of Turner, whom the narrator describes as an artist he admires. I am especially drawn in by Locksley's description of the ships and fort across the water. This painting evokes the same emotions for me. The New England setting with the fort in the background, and the boat in the harbor, reminds me of both the cove Locksley explores that afternoon before he is rescued by Captain Blunt, and the landscapes that he works on all those months.

A Wagner Matinee

Willa Cather, 1905

"A Wagner Matinee" begins with the narrator, Clark, receiving a letter announcing the imminent arrival of his Aunt Georgina. We can see that his previous impression is distaste and condescension for the older woman and the place she lives now. Her figure is "pathetic and grotesque," and the narrator becomes ill at ease remembering his time spent on her farm; even the letter itself is "none too clean" and his uncle "characteristically delayed writing" the letter.

And when Georgina arrives, her appearance has devolved (in Clark's mind). He compares her stooped figure and dusty traveling clothes to explorers who have lost limbs and are gaped at with "awe and respect" due to the hardships they have suffered. Although he uses complimentary words to describe this feeling, the reader is left with the impression that Clark feels sympathy for her current physical condition, which he calls "misshapen."

The narrative continues, describing Georgina's past as a music teacher and her decision to join her husband thirty years before as they began farming in Nebraska. Clark contrasts her former society life with her farm life, generally in disparaging terms. He doubts she has retained any of her former love of music, and he thinks she likely won't enjoy the concert he has booked for them to attend. In fact, he goes so far as to hope her taste in music has disappeared, assuming she will be unhappy with the deprivation of farm life after her former existence as a musician.

Georgina's reaction to the concert, from the moment they step into the hall, proves him wrong on all counts. Her passion for music comes rushing back to her, and Clark realizes he has misjudged her. He goes so far as to say the concert broke the flat and wasteful silence of her plains-and-farm life of thirty years.

While Clark may be correct in his impression of her reawakening, his insistence that her life as a farmer has caused her appreciation for music to disappear seems very classist. It's as though, unless people stay in a cultural epicenter like Boston, keeping their hands clean of dirt and farm work, they will lose their enjoyment of the arts.

This short story has been criticized as an unfair judgment of rural culture, but I think Cather is saying quite the opposite. Although high society may have believed it shameful to choose to leave a rich, artful city and begin a life on the plains of Nebraska, it is obvious through Georgina's stories of cowhands who sing to her, and her reaction to the Wagner concert, that this love and appreciation of music has never left her and probably never will. It is obvious that choosing to leave behind a life that is supposedly so rich and full of art, does not mean that a person's artistic life is necessarily over.

I have chosen *At the Piano*, sketched by Theodore Robinson circa 1887, to accompany this story. The young woman has a thoughtful look, as I can envision on the face of a contemplative Georgina as a teacher back in Boston, or in the present day, playing her parlor organ or listening to the farmhands sing in Nebraska while she attends to her farm duties. I am moved by this sketch because it's how I envision Aunt Georgina, how she must have looked in her younger days, at the piano. Although she's now an old woman who has spent her life mostly deprived of her greatest inspiration, her passion for music has never left her and has been kept alive in unexpected ways, including by farmhands who sing while they work. I imagine her emotions during the Wagner concert evoke this memory of herself as a young musician.

There are characters in each of these stories who have a bias toward the "artistic class." They, unlike the authors, believe that art is not accessible to or cannot be appreciated by all. The message in these stories is that you don't need to be educated in the arts, or an artist, or wealthy, or of a particular gender—you only need imagination to recognize art and beauty. You are here to read these stories with your background, your education, and your personal experience in the world at this time.

Genevieve Sheets
April 2019

A Point at Issue!

Kate Chopin

Originally appeared in St. Louis Post-Dispatch, *October 27, 1889.*

Married—On Tuesday, May 11, Eleanor Gail to Charles Faraday.

Nothing bearing the shape of a wedding announcement could have been less obtrusive than the foregoing hidden in a remote corner of the Plymdale *Promulgator*, clothed in the palest and smallest of type, and modestly wedged in between the big, black-lettered offer of the *Promulgator* to mail itself free of extra charge to subscribers leaving home for the summer months, and an equally somber-clad notice (doubtless astray as to place and application) that Hammersmith & Co. were carrying a large and varied assortment of marble and granite monuments!

Yet notwithstanding its sandwiched condition, that little marriage announcement seemed to Eleanor to parade the whole street.

Whichever way she turned her eyes, it glowered at her with scornful reproach.

She felt it to be an indelicate thrusting of herself upon the public notice; and at the sight she was plunged in regret at having made to the proprieties the concession of permitting it.

She hoped now that the period for making concessions was ended. She had endured long and patiently the trials that beset her path when she chose to diverge from the beaten walks of female Plymdaledom. Had stood stoically enough the questionable distinction of being relegated to a place amid that large and ill-assorted family of "cranks," feeling the discomfit and attending opprobrium to be far outbalanced by the satisfying consciousness of roaming the heights of free thought, and tasting the sweets of a spiritual emancipation.

The closing act of Eleanor's young ladyhood, when she chose to be married without pre-announcement, without the paraphernalia of accessories so dear to a curious public—had been in keeping with previous methods distinguishing her career. The disappointed public cheated of its entertainment, was forced to seek such compensation for the loss as was offered in reflections that while condemning her present, were unsparing of her past, and full with damning prognostic of her future.

Charles Faraday, who added to his unembellished title that of Professor of Mathematics of the Plymdale University, had found in Eleanor Gail his ideal woman.

Indeed, she rather surpassed that ideal, which had of

necessity been but an adorned picture of woman as he had known her. A mild emphasizing of her merits, a soft toning down of her defects had served to offer to his fancy a prototype of that bequoted creature.

"Not too good for human nature's daily food," yet so good that he had cherished no hope of beholding such a one in the flesh. Until Eleanor had come, supplanting his ideal, and making of that fanciful creation a very simpleton by contrast. In the beginning he had found her extremely good to look at, with her combination of graceful womanly charms, unmarred by self-conscious mannerisms that was as rare as it was engaging. Talking with her, he had caught a look from her eyes into his that he recognized at once as a free masonry of intellect. And the longer he knew her, the greater grew his wonder at the beautiful revelations of her mind that unfurled itself to his, like the curling petals of some hardy blossom that opens to the inviting warmth of the sun. It was not that Eleanor knew many things. According to her own modest estimate of herself, she knew nothing. There were school girls in Plymdale who surpassed her in the amount of their positive knowledge. But she was possessed of a clear intellect: sharp in its reasoning, strong and unprejudiced in its outlook. She was that *rara avis*, a logical woman—something which Faraday had not encountered in his life before. True, he was not hoary with age. At thirty the types of women he had met with were not legion; but he felt safe in doubting that the hedges of the future would grow logical women for him, more than they had borne such prodigies in the past.

He found Eleanor ready to take broad views of life and

humanity; able to grasp a question and anticipate conclusions by a quick intuition which he himself reached by the slower, consecutive steps of reason.

During the months that shaped themselves into the cycle of a year these two dwelt together in the harmony of a united purpose.

Together they went looking for the good things of life, knocking at the closed doors of philosophy; venturing into the open fields of science, she, with uncertain steps, made steady by his help.

Whithersoever he led she followed, oftentimes in her eagerness taking the lead into unfamiliar ways in which he, weighted with a lingering conservatism, had hesitated to venture.

So did they grow in their oneness of thought to belong each so absolutely to the other that the idea seemed not to have come to them that this union might be made faster by marriage. Until one day it broke upon Faraday, like a revelation from the unknown, the possibility of making her his wife.

When he spoke, eager with the new awakened impulse, she laughingly replied:

"Why not?" She had thought of it long ago.

In entering upon their new life they decided to be governed by no precedential methods. Marriage was to be a form, that while fixing legally their relation to each other, was in no wise to touch the individuality of either; that was to be preserved intact. Each was to remain a free integral of humanity, responsible to no dominating exactions of so-called marriage laws. And the element that was to make possible such a union was trust in each other's love, honor, courtesy, tempered by the reserving clause of readiness to meet the consequences of reciprocal liberty.

Faraday appreciated the need of offering to his wife advantages for culture which had been of impossible attainment during her girlhood.

Marriage, which marks too often the closing period of a woman's intellectual existence, was to be in her case the open portal through which she might seek the embellishments that her strong, graceful mentality deserved.

An urgent desire with Eleanor was to acquire a thorough speaking knowledge of the French language. They agreed that a lengthy sojourn in Paris could be the only practical and reliable means of accomplishing such an end.

Faraday's three months of vacation were to be spent by them in the idle happiness of a loitering honeymoon through the continent of Europe, then he would leave his wife in the French capital for a stay that might extend indefinitely—two, three years—as long as should be found needful, he returning to join her with the advent of each summer, to renew their love in a fresh and re-strengthened union.

And so, in May, they were married, and in September we find Eleanor established in the pension of the old couple Clairegobeau and comfortably ensconced in her pretty room that opened on to the Rue Rivoli, her heart full of sweet memories that were to cheer her coming solitude.

On the wall, looking always down at her with his quiet, kind glance, hung the portrait of her husband. Beneath it stood the fanciful little desk at which she hoped to spend many happy hours.

Books were everywhere, giving character to the graceful furnishings which their united taste had evolved from the paucity of the Clairegobeau germ, and out of the window was Paris!

Eleanor was supremely satisfied amid her new and attractive surroundings. The pang of parting from her husband seeming to lend sharp zest to a situation that offered the fulfillment of a cherished purpose.

Faraday, with the stronger man-nature, felt more keenly the discomfit of giving up a companionship that in its brief duration had been replete with the duality of accomplished delight and growing promise.

But to him also was the situation made acceptable by its involving a principle which he felt it incumbent upon him to uphold. He returned to Plymdale and to his duties at the university, and resumed his bachelor existence as quietly as though it had been interrupted but by the interval of a day.

The small public with which he had acquaintance, and which had forgotten his existence during the past few months, was fired anew with indignant astonishment at the effrontery of the situation which his singular coming back offered to their contemplation.

That two young people should presume to introduce such innovations into matrimony!

It was uncalled for!

It was improper!

It was indecent!

He must have already tired of her idiosyncrasies, since he had left her in Paris.

And in Paris, of all places, to leave a young woman alone! Why not at once in Hades?

She had been left in Paris forsooth to learn French. And since when was Mme. Belaire's French, as it had been taught to select generations of Plymdalions, considered insufficient for the practical needs of existence as related by that foreign tongue?

But Faraday's life was full with occupation and his brief moments of leisure were too precious to give to heeding the idle gossip that floated to his hearing and away again without holding his thoughts an instant.

He lived uninterruptedly a certain existence with his wife through the medium of letters. True, an inadequate substitute for her actual presence, but there was much satisfaction in this constant communion of thought between them.

They told such details of their daily lives as they thought worth the telling.

Their readings were discussed. Opinions exchanged. Newspaper cuttings sent back and forth, bearing upon questions that interested them. And what did not interest them?

Nothing was so large that they dare not look at it. Happenings, small in themselves, but big in their psychological comprehensiveness, held them with strange fascination. Her earnestness and intensity in such matters were extreme; but happily, Faraday brought to this union humorous instincts, and an optimism that saved it from a too monotonous sombreness.

The young man had his friends in Plymdale. Certainly none that ever remotely approached the position which Eleanor held in that regard. She stood pre-eminent. She was himself.

But his nature was genial. He invited companionship from his fellow beings, who, however short that companionship might be, carried always a gratifying consciousness of having made their personalities felt.

The society in Plymdale which he most frequented was that of the Beatons.

Beaton père was a fellow professor, many years older than Faraday, but one of those men with whom time, after putting its customary stamp upon his outward being, took no further care.

The spirit of his youth had remained untouched, and formed the nucleus around which the family gathered, drawing the light of their own cheerfulness.

Mrs. Beaton was a woman whose aspirations went not further than the desire for her family's good, and her bearing announced in its every feature, the satisfaction of completed hopes.

Of the daughters, Margaret, the eldest, was looked upon as slightly erratic, owing to a timid leaning in the direction of Woman's Suffrage.

Her activity in that regard, taking the form of a desultory correspondence with members of a certain society of protest; the fashioning and donning of garments of mysterious shape, which, while stamping their wearer with the distinction of a quasi-emancipation, defeated the ultimate purpose of their construction by inflicting a personal discomfort that extended beyond the powers of long endurance. Miss Kitty Beaton, the youngest daughter, and just returned from boarding school, while clamoring for no privileges doubtful of attainment and of remote and questionable benefit, with a Napoleonic grip, possessed herself of such rights as were at hand and exercised them in keeping the household under her capricious command.

She was at that age of blissful illusion when a girl is in love with her own youth and beauty and happiness. That age which heeds no purpose in the scope of creation further than may touch her majesty's enjoyment. Who would not smilingly endure with that charming selfishness of youth, knowing that the rough hand of experience is inevitably descending to disturb the short-lived dream?

They were all clever people, bright and interesting, and in this family circle Faraday found an acceptable relaxation from work and enforced solitude.

If they ever doubted the wisdom or expediency of his domestic relations, courtesy withheld the expression of any such doubts. Their welcome was always complete in its friendliness, and the interest which they evinced in the absent Eleanor proved that she was held in the highest esteem.

With Beaton Faraday enjoyed that pleasant intercourse which may exist between men whose ways, while not too divergent, are yet divided by an appreciable interval.

But it remained for Kitty to touch him with her girlish charms in a way, which, though not too usual with Faraday, meant so little to the man that he did not take the trouble to resent it.

Her laughter and song, the restless motions of her bubbling happiness, he watched with the casual pleasure that one follows the playful gambols of a graceful kitten.

He liked the soft shining light of her eyes. When she was near him the velvet smoothness of her pink cheeks stirred him with a feeling that could have found satisfying expression in a kiss.

It is idle to suppose that even the most exemplary men go through life with their eyes closed to woman's beauty and their senses steeled against its charm.

Faraday thought little of this feeling (and so should we if it were not outspoken).

In writing one day to his wife, with the cold-blooded impartiality of choosing a subject which he thought of neither more nor less prominence than the next, he descanted at some length upon the interesting emotions which Miss Kitty's pretty femininity aroused in him.

If he had given serious thought to the expediency of touching upon such a theme with one's wife, he still would not have been deterred. Was not Eleanor's large comprehensiveness far above the littleness of ordinary women?

Did it not enter into the scheme of their lives, to keep free from prejudices that hold their sway over the masses?

But he thought not of that, for, after all, his interest in Kitty and his interest in his university class bore about an equal reference to Eleanor and his love for her.

His letter was sent, and he gave no second thought to the matter of its contents.

The months went by for Faraday with few distinctive features to mark them outside the enduring desire for his wife's presence.

There had been a visit of sharp disturbance once when her customary letter failed him, and the tardy missive coming, carried an inexplicable coldness that dealt him a pain which, however, did not long survive a little judicious reflection and a very deluge of letters from Paris that shook him with their unusual ardor.

May had come again, and at its approach Faraday with the impatience of a hundred lovers hastened across the seas to join his Eleanor.

It was evening and Eleanor paced to and fro in her room, making the last of a series of efforts that she had been putting forth all day to fight down a misery of the heart, against which her reason was in armed rebellion. She had tried the strategy of simply ignoring its presence, but the attempt had failed utterly. During her daily walk it had embodied itself in every object that her eyes rested upon. It had enveloped her like a smoke mist, through which Paris looked more dull than the desolation of Sahara.

She had thought to displace it with work, but, like the disturbing element in the chemist's crucible, it rose again and again overspreading the surface of her labor.

Alone in her room, the hour had come when she meant to succeed by the unaided force of reason—proceeding first to make herself bodily comfortable in the folds of a majestic flowing gown, in which she looked a distressed goddess.

Her hair hung heavy and free about her shoulders, for

those reasoning powers were to be spurred by a plunging of white fingers into the golden mass.

In this dishevelled state Eleanor's presence seemed too large for the room and its delicate furnishings. The place fitted well an Eleanor in repose but not an Eleanor who swept the narrow confines like an incipient cyclone.

Reason did good work and stood its ground bravely, but against it were the too great odds of a woman's heart, backed by the soft prejudices of a far-reaching heredity.

She finally sank into a chair before her pretty writing desk. The golden head fell upon the outspread arms waiting to receive it, and she burst into a storm of sobs and tears. It was the signal of surrender.

It is a gratifying privilege to be permitted to ignore the reason of such unusual disturbance in a woman of Eleanor's high qualifications. The cause of that abandonment of grief will never be learned unless she chooses to disclose it herself.

When Faraday first folded his wife in his arms he saw but the Eleanor of his constant dreams. But he soon began to perceive how more beautiful she had grown; with a richness of coloring and fullness of health that Plymdale had never been able to bestow. And the object of her stay in Paris was gaining fast to accomplishment, for she had already acquired a knowledge of French that would not require much longer to perfect.

They sat together in her room discussing plans for the summer, when a timid knock at the door caused Eleanor to look up, to see the little housemaid eyeing her with the

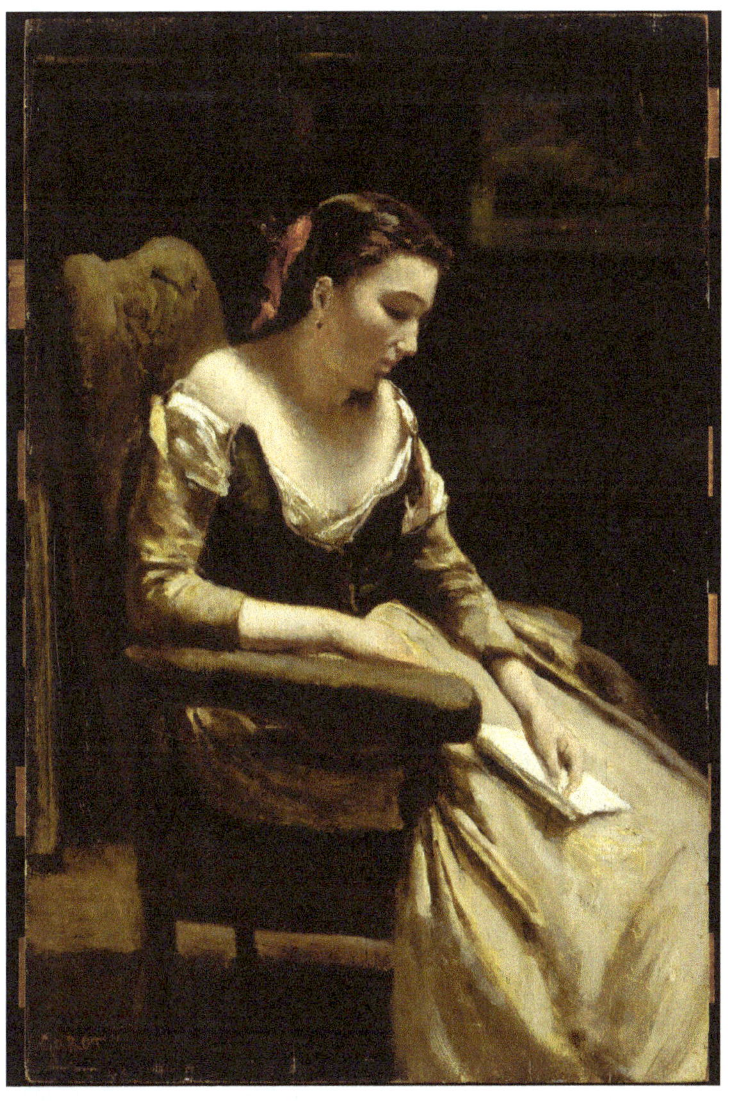

Camille Corot, *The Letter*, ca. 1865, The Metropolitan Museum of Art, New York, H. O. Havemeyer Collection, Gift of Horace Havemeyer, 1929

glance of a fellow conspirator and holding in her hand a card that she suffered to be but partly visible.

Eleanor hastily approached her, and reading the name upon the card thrust it into her pocket, exchanging some whispered words with the girl, among which were audible, "excuse me," "engaged," "another time." She came back to her husband looking a little flustered, to resume the conversation where it had been interrupted and he offered no inquiries about her mysterious caller.

Entering the salon not many days later he found that in doing so he interrupted a conversation between his wife and a very striking looking gentleman who seemed on the point of taking his leave.

They were both disconcerted; she especially, in bowing, almost thrusting him out, had the appearance of wanting to run away; to do any thing but meet her husband's glance.

He asked with assumed indifference who her friend might be.

"Oh, no one special," with a hopeless attempt at brazenness.

He accepted the situation without protest, only indulging the reflection that Eleanor was losing something of her frankness.

But when his wife asked him on another occasion to dispense with her company for a whole afternoon, saying that she had an urgent call upon her time, he began to wonder if there might not be modifications to this marital liberty of which he was so staunch an advocate.

She left him with a hundred little endearments that she seemed to have acquired with her French.

He forced himself to the writing of a few urgent letters, but his restlessness did not permit him to do more.

It drove him to ugly thoughts, then to the means of dispelling them.

He gazed out of the window, wondered why he was remaining indoors, and followed up the reflection by seizing his hat and plunging out into the street.

The Paris boulevards of a day in early summer are calculated to dispel almost any ache but one of that nature, which was making itself incipiently felt with Faraday.

It was at that stage when it moves a man to take exception at the inadequacy of everything that is offered to his contemplation or entertainment.

The sun was too hot.

The shop windows were vulgar; lacking artistic detail in their make-up.

How could he ever have found the Paris women attractive? They had lost their chic. Most of them were scrawny—not worth looking at.

He thought to go and stroll through the galleries of art. He knew Eleanor would wish to be with him; then he was tempted to go alone.

Finally, more tired from inward than outward restlessness, he took refuge at one of the small tables of a café, called for a "Mazarin," and, so seated for an unheeded time, let the panorama of Paris pass before his indifferent eyes.

When suddenly one of the scenes in this shifting show struck him with stunning effect.

It was the sight of his wife riding in a fiacre with her caller of a few days back, both conversing and in high spirits.

He remained for a moment enervated, then the blood came tingling back into his veins like fire, making his finger ends twitch with a desire (full worthy of any one of the "prejudiced masses") to tear the scoundrel from his seat and paint the boulevard red with his villainous blood.

A rush of wild intentions crowded into his brain.

Should he follow and demand an explanation? Leave Paris without ever looking into her face again? and more not worthy of the man.

It is right to say that his better self and better senses came quickly back to him.

That first revolt was like the unwilling protest of the flesh against the surgeon's knife before a man has steeled himself to its endurance.

Everything came back to him from their short, common past—their dreams, their large intentions for the shaping of their lives. Here was the first test, and should he be the one to cry out, "I cannot endure it."

When he returned to the pension, Eleanor was impatiently waiting for him in the entry, radiant with gladness at his coming.

She was under a suppressed excitement that prevented her noting his disturbed appearance.

She took his listless hand and led him into the small drawing-room that adjoined their sleeping chamber.

There stood her companion of the fiacre, smiling as was she at the pleasure of introducing him to another Eleanor disposed on the wall in the best possible light to display the gorgeous radiance of her wonderful beauty and the skill of the man who had portrayed it.

The most sanguine hopes of Eleanor and her artist could not have anticipated anything like the rapture with which Faraday received this surprise.

"Monsieur l'Artiste" went away with his belief in the undemonstrativeness of the American very much shaken; and in his pocket substantial evidence of American appreciation of art.

Then the story was told how the portrait was intended as a surprise for his arrival. How there had been delay in its completion. The artist had required one more sitting, which she gave him that day, and the two had brought the picture home in the fiacre, he to give it the final advantages of a judicious light; to witness its effect upon Mons. Faraday and finally the excusable wish to be presented to the husband of the lady who had captivated his deepest admiration and esteem.

"You shall take it home with you," said Eleanor.

Both were looking at the lovely creation by the soft light of a reckless expenditure of bougie.

"Yes, dearest," he answered, with feeble elation at the prospect of returning home with that exquisite piece of inanimation.

"Have you engaged your return passage?" she asked.

She sat at his knee, arrayed in the gown that had one evening clothed such a goddess in distress.

"Oh, no. There's plenty time for that," was his answer. "Why do you ask?"

"I'm sure I don't know," and after a while:

"Charlie, I think—I mean, don't you think—I have made wonderful progress in French?"

"You've done marvels, Nellie. I find no difference between your French and Mme. Clairegobeau's, except that yours is far prettier."

"Yes?" she rejoined, with a little squeeze of the hand.

"I mayn't be right and I want you to give me your candid opinion. I believe Mme. Belaire—now that I have gone so far—don't you think—hadn't you better engage passage for two?"

His answer took the form of a pantomimic rapture of assenting gratefulness, during which each gave speechless assurance of a love that could never more take a second place.

"Nellie," he asked, looking into the face that nestled in close reach of his warm kisses, "I have often wanted to know, though you needn't tell it if it doesn't suit you," he added, laughing, "why you once failed to write to me, and then sent a letter whose coldness gave me a week's heart trouble?"

She flushed, and hesitated, but finally answered him bravely, "It was when—when you cared so much for that Kitty Beaton."

Astonishment for a moment deprived him of speech.

"But Eleanor! In the name of reason! It isn't possible!"

"I know all you would say," she replied, "I have been over the whole ground myself, over and over, but it is useless.

I have found that there are certain things which a woman can't philosophize about, any more than she can about death when it touches that which is near to her."

"But you don't think—"

"Hush! don't speak of it ever again. I think nothing!" closing her eyes, and with a little shudder drawing closer to him.

As he kissed his wife with passionate fondness, Faraday thought, "I love her none the less for it, but my Nellie is only a woman, after all."

With man's usual inconsistency, he had quite forgotten the episode of the portrait.

Wade's Technique

Maryann D'Agincourt

First published in All Most *by Portmay Press, 2013.*

I

"You were in a dark place," she paused, then said, "Gregory."

Her voice was pensive, though he heard a slight edge in it when she spoke his name. He watched Sheila lower her head with exacting grace and look away from him.

Reluctantly he waited for her to say more.

It was early August and the air-conditioning in his high-ceilinged apartment was not working because of a power failure. All the windows had been opened to the unrelenting sound of city traffic.

Her narrow form was perfectly framed by the long window. Late afternoon light poured into the room, brightening her hazy gray eyes. Again their gazes met. Though her expression was impassive, her arms were extended in disbelief. She continued: "I believe you were in a cave. The dream was in black and white, not color."

Gregory, his heart thumping, crossed his arms and moved closer, assessing her as if she were a physician providing a review of his health.

Her face was damp from the heat; the more she spoke, the more her wide-set eyes appeared spread apart. He found her voice prickly; she paused, as if each word contained a meaning separate from the sentence as a whole.

He looked past her, out the open window, at the concrete apartment buildings lining the street, and then at the stalled cars below, horns blaring into the fog of heat. And he envisioned the very same street last winter—how often cars had been just as immobilized but because of the snow—and his thoughts then drifted to the unexpected February storm. He and Sheila had spent the day together, doing errands, skating, and then dining at an Italian restaurant. When they had returned to her apartment, she had snapped open the blinds, and with lights off they'd sat on the sofa, mostly in silence, sharing a bottle of tequila, watching the thick white flakes fall profusely from the black sky. "How overwhelming," she said, her words echoing into the darkness.

"I find it calming," he responded, reflexively taking another gulp of liquor.

An hour later he studied her, the lights now on and dimmed; she waltzed about the room in that graceful-sharp way of hers, clutching the tequila bottle close to her chest, casting shadows about the room. Her usual reserved expression was animated and her hair, which she mostly wore in a French braid, was loosened, a dark, curly mass falling past her shoulders.

What proceeded, or what occurred following their first attempt at lovemaking that night, he could not recall. All he knew was that it had not happened again. They kept in contact, he guessed, because they were lonely, desirous.

"You were stuck, you couldn't move, perhaps it was mud—something viscous," she now said, raising one hand and rubbing two fingers together. She looked quizzically at him, as if expecting him to know the answer, he thought.

He uncrossed his arms and turned away, wondering what she wasn't telling him about the dream—maybe she had dreamed he had drowned in quicksand. Disquieted, he ignored her words and focused on her presence. Despite her dispassion, which he, a Midwesterner, had found inherent in other New Englanders as well, he believed she was different, ultimately hopeful.

She had called him a few hours before and had said she wanted to stop by after she finished her work at the studio. He had been discomforted by her voice; she had sounded as if she intended to relay bad news to him.

"I did not know whether or not you needed help getting out of this cave. But I think that was only the center of the dream. I'm not sure, that's what is so confusing about it," she said, raising her brows. But he believed she appeared more perspicacious than confused.

"The dream was strong, visceral. I needed to see you today, to see if you were well." She paused, and for a moment, he saw angst in her expression, yet heard a subtle tone of relief in her voice, not because he was fine, he thought, but because she had felt some sort of responsibility in telling him about the dream.

Not knowing what to make of her dream—he had always felt dissatisfied discussing someone's dreams, or recalling his own—he changed the subject. He scratched his head and told her he had been thinking of going to a movie, to escape inside an air-conditioned theater.

"I'll come with you," Sheila answered solemnly. But he thought she seemed preoccupied with the dream.

As they walked toward the cinema he effortlessly took her hand, pressing her palm, flecked with dry paint, against his. Glancing at him, Sheila began to speak about Adam Wade, a contemporary artist known for his fine surreal landscapes. She told him a show of his would be coming to Boston in a few weeks. A balmy breeze draped a strand of loose hair across her forehead. Gray clouds appeared, and the sky was darkening quickly, suddenly. He was accustomed to her choosing a topic of conversation she knew he would disagree with and then relentlessly pursuing it.

In one quick breath he said that, as he had mentioned to her before, he had seen the artist's work and had found Wade's paintings to be desolate—hopeless—maybe bland.

Sliding her hand from his grasp, Sheila said she disagreed. She believed Wade was an expansive, innovative artist.

She walked a few paces ahead, one shoulder slightly raised. He felt a raindrop on his arm, then heard thunder in the distance; within minutes there was a downpour, water streaming down the street.

Instead of continuing in the direction of the cinema, they turned and ran in the opposite direction, back toward his apartment.

In his small kitchen he stood next to the window, the sill damp from the rain, water vigorously striking the pane. He turned away and reached for a bottle of wine from the top shelf; he heard Sheila moving about the living room, the heels of her shoes clacking against the hardwood floor.

Droplets of rain from his hair sprinkled the floor as he lowered his head and poured the wine, filling two glasses to the brim.

Eyeing Sheila through the doorway, he watched her sit on the brown corduroy sofa, cross her legs, knot them tightly together, and lean forward. She caught his stare and in response she returned to their conversation about Wade.

"It's Wade's technique," she said. "It is what I most appreciate about his work. Fine strokes, faint colors, provocative, compelling—his complexity lies in his simplicity, his ability to accept his simplicity."

"Is acceptance a propensity, or an ability?" Gregory asked as he came toward her and handed her a glass of wine. She looked up at him; he saw the black flecks in her eyes contract, her lashes moist, steady, the faint lines on her forehead more evident.

"The latter," she answered decidedly. Pausing, she asked him if he'd like to go with her to the Wade exhibit. He nodded. A truce of sorts, he thought.

He sat next to her, placed the bottle of wine on the floor, then turned halfway round and reached behind the sofa for

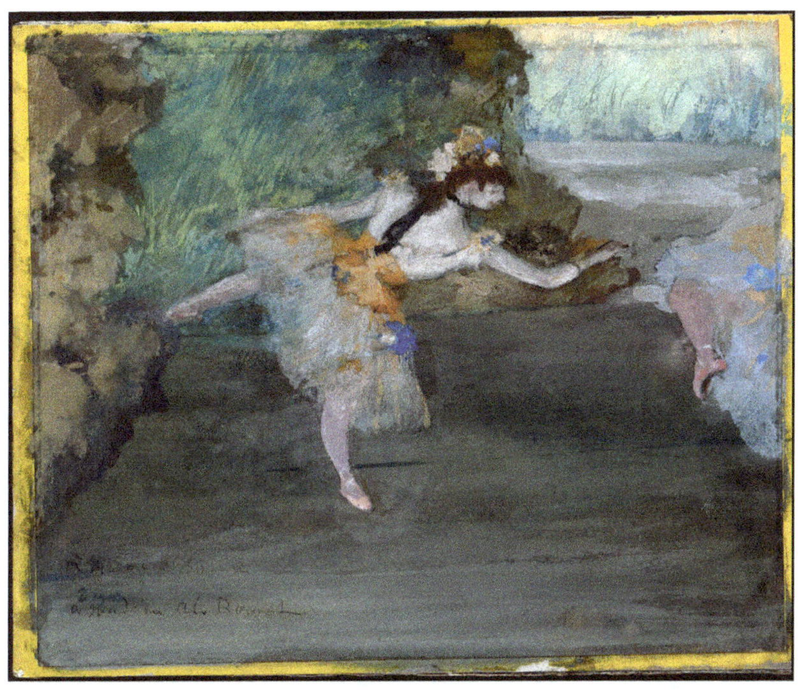

Edgar Degas, *Dancer Onstage*, ca. 1877, The Metropolitan Museum of Art, New York, The Lesley and Emma Sheafer Collection, Bequest of Emma A. Sheafer, 1973

a small pile of CDs lying on the table next to the player. He carefully placed one inside the machine. Soon jazz filtered through the room.

Glancing over at Sheila, he saw she was staring straight ahead, intently sipping her wine. Then she half smiled and raised her glass for more. Was she silently debating their conversation about Wade, or their very odd relationship? he wondered, pouring more wine into her glass.

The rich and complicated sound of Miles Davis on trumpet filled the room. Water pelted the windowpane. And soon under the spell of the thick, red wine and the heavy rain, they slid into one another's arms, then legs.

The next day, he woke early. Before him, Sheila was perfunctorily dressing, zipping up her jean shorts, stretching her arms through the holes of a sleeveless cotton jersey.

Abruptly he sat up in bed, gazing at her quick, neat movements. The bright morning light grazed the top of her head; her naturally curly hair now had a static electric look.

Their gazes locked; Sheila returned to their conversation of the previous night. She spoke about Wade, going to the exhibit—which day would be best for him? Gregory heard himself respond to her in kind.

Grasping our way back to friendship, he thought, like two people slowly, awkwardly climbing onto separate rafts after having been out dunking together in murky waters.

She told him she wanted to get to the studio early, before the heat set in.

In his bathrobe, he walked her to the door, his bare feet

against the rough floor. Standing on the threshold, he gently kissed her.

He went to the window and watched her amble down the street, like a dancer in toe shoes, stepping forward on the heels of her feet. He had seen that walk before.

II

Fifteen summers earlier, twenty-year-old Gregory, following a semester of studying Dutch history in Amsterdam, had traveled on his own throughout much of Europe.

After spending the last few weeks of May in France, he had boarded a train to Berlin and then made his way west. Four days later, he arrived in a north German town. After two days there, in the June twilight, he walked slowly toward the train station. A few feet ahead he noticed a woman with a backpack and camera bag, walking on her heels, like a ballerina. But he soon lost sight of her.

After purchasing his ticket, he sat on the concrete platform, his backpack at his side, and waited for the train. Across the tracks he saw a band of four accordion players who had emerged, it seemed, from nowhere. Without introduction they began to play hollow, discordant-sounding music.

For a moment Gregory felt lost. To orient himself, he turned away, and saw that next to him was the woman who had been walking ahead of him moments before.

When she noticed him looking at her, she stared directly at him, not flinching. Her eyes were a deep brown without any specks of light, her chin narrow and firm. She asked if he was an American.

"Yes," he said. She shifted her body so that she was now facing him, then tilted her head to the side, her eyes attentive.

She told him she was from this town, from north Germany, and, pointing to her camera bag, she added that she studied photography. Was he traveling south? Before he had a chance to answer, she told him her name was Karin. She leaned forward and said in her fine English, "It is spelled with an *i*."

Their first night together they spent in a Munich inn run by a tall woman in her late fifties, strongly built. As they checked in Gregory noticed the proprietress wore a Playboy bunny–shaped key dangling from a long silver chain round her neck, resting atop her full chest. Her English was good, but heavily accented. When she placed the key to the room in Gregory's palm, her hand felt coarse, and he took note of her haughty expression. After taking a few steps, Karin at his side, he looked back and saw that the proprietress now appeared wistful. He was disoriented—was her necklace an omen of some sort?

Over the next few days, whenever he saw the proprietress checking someone in at the front desk or clearing coffee cups in the hotel lobby, the bunny key dangling from the chain, he forced himself to ignore her strong back, her tight, firm movements.

Gregory never parted from Karin during the two and a

half weeks they spent together. Her stark honesty was what he liked best about her. And there was her dark, shiny hair, her long bangs looping over her brows, her naturally sallow coloring, her intense expression made more so by her high cheekbones and narrow chin.

They would sit naked together on the hard, small bed. He would feel more exposed than Karin, as if his whole being was splayed out, while she would sit with her knees raised, her crossed arms gracefully covering her breasts.

They would discuss what they were each looking for in life, how everything was spread out in front of them. "Possible, yet impossible," Karin said, drawing back her head.

He told her his parents were philosophy professors, but that because of this or perhaps in opposition to it, he was a realist. He spoke with his hands, making strong jerky movements; he had never felt more earnest.

One rainy afternoon he allowed Karin to photograph him, his nakedness. She was intent and exacting as she instructed him on how to pose.

A few days later, on an unseasonably cool night, they retired early to their room. She sat on the bed reading a photography magazine with a picture of the Taj Mahal on the cover, while he lay on the floor, his back against the rough surface; he held open a book about Florence and the Medici family. He would be heading to Italy in three days, hoping for warmer weather.

Karin suddenly looked up, pushed aside her bangs, and caught his gaze. She spoke directly, dispassionately. "Gregory, what is it that irks you?"

He was startled, but not by her question. What surprised him was the tone of her voice. It touched him, pierced into him as if he were being given a needle by an expert phlebotomist.

He looked at her, forcing his voice to sound as dispassionate as hers, and said, "I do not want to be who I am."

"Not be who you are," she repeated, as if urging him to say more.

He saw she was intrigued.

He continued to speak, fearful that if he stopped, or his tone changed, the mood between them would dissipate.

He told her he had a disease of the temperament—passivity—and explained how he believed he was lost, how he had never really connected with anyone in his life. He was afraid he would simply drift away because that was what happened to people like him. He was moving through life, detached and alone. He had come to Europe to rid himself of this passivity. But nothing had changed. He still was who he was. His temperament was as slow and as uneventful as a waltz.

When he finished speaking, Karin looked at him in that direct way of hers, the night outside growing darker, her face seeming more and more distant. She went to him and caressed his face with her long fingers, cold, assuring. "No. You are not simply moving through life, you have substance, you are my lover," she whispered.

For years he would recall her words, never fully realizing the effect they had had on him at the time or the effect they would have on him in the future.

"I have a temperament problem," he would say, wringing his hands, to each therapist he went to for his usual first and only session, and then he would repeat Karin's words to him or her: "You are my lover." Saying those words was an anodyne, temporarily relieving him of his angst.

On the night before they parted, Karin told Gregory she did not want to separate from him, that she loved him. She spoke in that too-serious way of hers.

Gregory felt angry, not knowing why or when his anger toward her had begun. At first he thought it was because he had revealed so much of himself to her. He was the one who had sat naked on the bed while she had seductively draped her arms round her body. What would she do with those photographs of him? Would they be out there for all to see? Or, when she eventually realized he had no intention of pursuing the relationship, would she fling them out her window? He imagined pictures of his naked self floating in the air before touching ground.

He promised to write and see her again soon, maybe next year. But he knew he would never again contact her. When she wasn't in sight, he had torn up her phone number and address to prove to himself he was serious.

He sensed Karin's melancholy when they parted, as if she knew what he had been thinking, feeling.

A week later, at the Uffizi Gallery in Florence, standing before Botticelli's *Birth of Venus*, he felt a sudden pang for Karin. He was raw inside, as if he had lost part of himself.

He wanted to call her, realizing he had been too rational. But he was unable to reach her. He could not remember the correct spelling of her family name. He tried different spellings. But nobody knew her wherever he called. Perhaps her number was not listed. He hadn't thought she would be difficult to find when he had confidently, justifiably ripped up her name and address. But he had done it with finality; he had not wanted to be able to reach her.

He caught a plane to Frankfurt, then took a train to the small town where they had met, to see if she would reappear. It was in the middle of the afternoon, and the four accordion players were there, playing that hollow-sounding music. Gregory continued to look about the station for Karin. He was young, he kept telling himself; he would survive the pain, the amputation.

III

Gregory Budowski had met Sheila Gerard two months shy of his thirty-third birthday. She was the temporary replacement for the full-time art teacher who was on maternity leave. Each morning he would watch Sheila walk quickly up the front steps of the looming brick building, carrying a canvas bag filled with construction paper and paintbrushes she had purchased for her students. They would both arrive at the same time, earlier than most of the other teachers.

Sheila told him she needed to get to school early because she had to do the lesson planning she should have done the previous day. She could not afford to lose the afternoon light, so she left school soon after the final bell sounded to go to her studio and paint.

Gregory told her he was there at seven thirty to do his lesson planning too. But he did not add that after he left the high school in the early afternoon, he would forget about his work and students and ride the subway into Cambridge, sit in a café; over an espresso he would pretend to read a newspaper or magazine or he would listen in on other people's conversations while contemplating his past failed relationships. With few exceptions, he was unable to clearly recall the features of any women he had known. He could only recreate blurred facial images, like off-center photographs. He would think of his ineptitude, his rash judgments, and then the pain his mistakes had caused others and himself. His blunders were ever present and clear in his mind, in his being; they had become a part of him.

Why had things never turned out quite the way he wanted them to? Each relationship had begun with so much hope. He wasn't certain what love was; he had silently aspired to it, but it had always eluded him.

Sometimes he wondered if he had been trying to punish himself all these years—for what, he wasn't certain—when he thought he had been seeking love.

He would let those thoughts roam about his mind for a moment and then drop them, as if they were reckless, vicious ideas he did not want to admit having because in some way they had given him a sense of comfort, perhaps pleasure. Then he would take a gulp of espresso, warily eyeing the people at the next table, as if they had been privy to his thoughts.

One Friday in late May, Gregory approached Sheila; she

was sitting alone in the dark, windowless teachers' room, browsing through an art magazine, sipping coffee from a disposable cup. He shrugged and asked if she would like to go for a drink with him later that afternoon.

Without looking at him, she placed the cup back on the table and said sure, after she finished at the studio.

Gregory picked her up at five o'clock. They drove past worn brick buildings with zigzagging fire escapes, the warm spring air billowing through the open windows. Finally he pulled up in front of a restaurant with a lounge.

He sat across from Sheila in a booth next to a bay window. The bright green leaves of an oak brushed against the glass, heavily shadowing the table and seats. Whenever she inclined her head to the side, or raised her hand to her cheek, he felt as if he were observing her from a distance as she maneuvered through covering shadows.

She didn't say anything after they ordered; she sat there, her hands folded, vaguely smiling, her thoughts elsewhere, he assumed. It struck him how shallow his knowledge of her was. To break the silence he asked her a simple question, an obvious one. Why art? He leaned forward, his gaze meeting her uncertain gray eyes.

Unclasping her hands, she furrowed her brows and told him in a tight, succinct voice that her father had died when she was fourteen. He had worked in a post office, and he had died right there on the job. He was sorting mail when a heavy instrument from a shelf above had fallen on his head. A freak accident, she said.

The spring following his death she had gone with her

class to the art museum. She had always liked to draw, but had never been inside an art museum before. She had been feeling sad, depressed, older than her classmates—they all seemed so happy, so free.

When she studied the paintings she saw movement—a woman's gown rustling, the heavy breathing of a man pulling a cart. From that point on, on most Saturday mornings, she would take a bus and then a subway into the city to go to the museum.

Her mother had worked during the day as a bank teller, and every night, after bidding Sheila a stoic good evening, she would shuffle off to bed in her furry gray slippers, holding the latest romance novel she was reading in one hand, and a glass of wine in the other.

Gregory was impressed with Sheila's story and wondered why he had never needed to immerse himself in anything. Though his childhood had not been touched by tragedy as Sheila's had, it had not been a very comforting one. Neither of his parents had been very relaxed in the presence of their two children, and although they were in the same field, they were not particularly compatible. And so they had obsessively thrown themselves into their work, creating a vacuum for him and his older sister. Yet Sheila—she had had such a harsh background, and had transcended her past. Hadn't she?

He responded by saying that maybe they could go to the museum together. He liked Turner.

He would call Sheila every few weeks. Often reticently, sometimes willingly, she would say yes, yes she would like to see him. At first Gregory wanted to be with her because he was hoping some part of her would rub off on him. She savored life more than he did. Lately he had found himself becoming more and more resigned.

One morning in the teachers' room, as he was placing his lunch in the refrigerator, Sheila said, out of the blue, "Gregory, you try too hard!" Startled, he was overcome by her words; he thought the opposite was true—he believed he did not try at all.

He thought she enjoyed visiting the museum with him, asking him his impressions of the paintings, telling him how she felt about what she saw. And he was beginning to understand what she meant when she spoke about seeing movement in a painting. It wasn't as farfetched as he first assumed. It was something he could grasp intellectually, but could not experience visually. "It has to do with both imagination and reality," Sheila explained. "You must use your imagination to see the reality of the painting—the artist's stroke, although it ends on canvas, continues on in the painter's mind, creating a sense of motion."

"A virtual reality," Gregory answered assuredly.

She placed her hands firmly on her hips and said, "No, it has nothing to do with computers," as if computers were the enemy, he thought. But they weren't. They were undeniably the fabric of society. Was she living in the past? he wondered. Was she immune to technology? But that was what had drawn him to her, he acknowledged; she represented the painful, solid past as well as the chaotic present.

IV

It was now mid-August, late in the afternoon. Drowsy from the heat and mug of beer he hastily drank at the museum café an hour before, Gregory lowered himself onto the leather sofa, half watching Sheila; she was moving about her apartment, hoisting open windows. Extending his arms across the back of the sofa, he sank his head into the crinkly fabric, giving her his full groggy attention. It struck him that he had been seeing Sheila for a little over two years, and he frankly did not know her.

All the windows in her third-floor apartment were now open, but there was still no breeze. Tilting his head, he studied her halter dress, how it clung to her, like a loose, moist bandage. As he closed his eyes, his desire for her, thumping and inconsistent, surfaced.

Ice cubes clacking against glass broke the warm silence in the room. He realized she was in the kitchen. She had vanished soundlessly, without leaving a trace, like a ghost.

Now there she was standing in the doorway, each hand clutching a buoying glass of sangria by the stem, sunlight flickering across her form, her mouth open, awed from the heat.

She placed one glass on the oak coffee table, and he watched expectantly as she extended her bare arm, handing him the other glass. As he took it, he felt the wet from her hand.

"Taste it," she said, insistently.

He pressed the glass to his mouth and sipped, gazing up at her.

As Gregory drank, Sheila eased herself downward, sat on the floor, tucked her knees under the table, nestled her pointy elbows against the wooden surface, raised the glass to her lips. They had made love a few weeks before, he thought. Now it seemed so unreal.

Her shoulders dropped forward and she pressed her forehead with the palm of her hand. "I've been hoping to set up a show for the fall," she said directly, "but it's not going very smoothly. This new critic in town has judged my oils harshly. He's awful. My work, he says, is precise and static, more like a waltz than a sonata."

"I like your work, Sheila," Gregory said, hovering over her, waiting for her to lift her head; he focused on wisps of hair swirling at the nape of her neck. "I don't think it's static—it is quite energetic, if you really look at it." But she still refused to look up at him.

He thought about the painting of hers he liked most, the painting of a cracked egg, the background misty, surreal—yes, still, but haunting, discomforting. He found solace in this, in her stillness.

Slightly raising her head, she peered into the hollow of the glass, fingering the rim. Though she had not moved, he felt as if she had walked away from him. And he knew it was time for him to leave.

"More sangria?" she asked. Shadows wobbled across the table; the sun was lowering, the heat relentless.

"No, I have to go," he said.

There was no elevator in the building, so he ambled down the worn marble stairs.

The sky slowly darkening, the heat a formless presence facing him, he strode toward his car, parked three blocks away. He was angry, very angry that Sheila was holding back from him. He would never see her again, he promised himself. But he knew, despite his anger, this was unrealistic; being with her, watching her stark, hopeful movements, gratified and reassured him.

A Friday afternoon, early September; it was the end of the first week of school. Gregory closed the classroom door behind him. He made his way down the dark, empty corridor. As he went toward the side exit, he came upon two students embracing, jammed in a narrow space between metal lockers—arms, bodies frenetically entwined; he caught a glimpse of the young woman's face, her expression of raw passion, and he was pained. He didn't say anything to them, just kept walking.

As he opened the door, he heard a gasp, and then "Budowski," his name, as if he was the enemy, staid, set in his ways, personally incomplete, beyond understanding what they were experiencing. He felt empty inside, then a deep ache.

The next morning, a Saturday, he woke early. He peered out the kitchen window: brief signs of autumn were beginning to show, trees wavering sporadically from a gust of cool air now and then, a single yellow leaf on an otherwise full, green tree.

He reached inside his pocket for his phone, and pressed Sheila's cell number.

Did she want to go for a ride—enjoy whatever was left of summer? he asked. He was feeling incredibly tired, tired of her, tired of his life.

Sheila suggested he come to her apartment.

When she opened the door, she was holding the cell phone to her ear. Motioning for him to come in, she walked to the other side of the room.

He remained in the doorway, studied her back, how erect her shoulders were as she haltingly spoke into the phone. She's discouraged today, he thought. He overheard bits and pieces of the conversation, and he realized an exhibit of her work she so desperately hoped to put together would probably not materialize.

"If you don't mind, I'd like to go to the museum," she said, putting her phone down on the coffee table.

"Really?" he asked, avoiding her gaze.

As they climbed the steps into the museum, Sheila told him she first wanted to see Degas.

They walked from room to room, crossing the parquet floors without stopping until they reached the Degas room. He followed her as she moved swiftly toward the painting of a lone dancer.

He stood behind her, waiting while she studied it. He was feeling restless, uncomfortable, confined by the museum—he would rather be outdoors, playing tennis. The museum felt empty, hollow, old, he thought.

She turned toward him. "Gregory," she said, her clear, definite voice piercing him. "I've lost something. I cannot see the movement anymore."

Then she reached up and drew her arms round his neck.

Uneasy, he wondered if she had not been honest with him. He placed his hands on her arms and took a slight step backward, hoping to slip away from her embrace. Not knowing where to look, his eyes fastened on the painting of the Degas dancer. The dancer's extended arm formed a semicircle and as Gregory watched he imagined it rising, as if to stop him. His gaze locked on the painting, he could not move; it was as if it were all those years ago and he was sitting in that north German train station, looking up at the musicians on the platform.

He recalled the hollow-sounding music, and how on the surface he had been uncertain, anxious, every so often he had glanced around, his eyes straining for Karin, hoping to catch a glimpse of her haunted but kind expression. Though within he had begun to grow calm, expectant; he thought he had taken a step forward by returning to that spot, searching for her, fully believing his life in some way was only beginning.

The Portrait

Edith Wharton

First published in The Greater Inclination *by Charles Scribner's Sons, 1899.*

It was at Mrs. Mellish's, one Sunday afternoon last spring. We were talking over George Lillo's portraits—a collection of them was being shown at Durand-Ruel's—and a pretty woman had emphatically declared:—

"Nothing on earth would induce me to sit to him!"

There was a chorus of interrogations.

"Oh, because—he makes people look so horrid; the way one looks on board ship, or early in the morning, or when one's hair is out of curl and one knows it. I'd so much rather be done by Mr. Cumberton!"

Little Cumberton, the fashionable purveyor of rose-water pastels, stroked his moustache to hide a conscious smile.

"Lillo is a genius—that we must all admit," he said indulgently, as though condoning a friend's weakness; "but he has an unfortunate temperament. He has been denied the gift—so precious to an artist—of perceiving the ideal. He sees only the defects of his sitters; one might almost fancy that he takes a morbid pleasure in exaggerating their weak points, in painting them on their worst days; but I honestly believe he can't help himself. His peculiar limitations prevent his seeing anything but the most prosaic side of human nature—

"'*A primrose by the river's brim*
A yellow primrose is to him,
And it is nothing more.'"

Cumberton looked round to surprise an order in the eye of the lady whose sentiments he had so deftly interpreted, but poetry always made her uncomfortable, and her nomadic attention had strayed to other topics. His glance was tripped up by Mrs. Mellish.

"Limitations? But, my dear man, it's because he hasn't any limitations, because he doesn't wear the portrait-painter's conventional blinders, that we're all so afraid of being painted by him. It's not because he sees only one aspect of his sitters, it's because he selects the real, the typical one, as instinctively as a detective collars a pick-pocket in a crowd. If there's nothing to paint—no real person—he paints nothing; look at the sumptuous emptiness of his portrait of Mrs. Guy Awdrey"—("Why," the pretty woman perplexedly interjected, "that's the only nice picture he ever did!") "If there's one positive trait in a negative whole he brings it out in spite of himself; if it isn't a nice trait, so much the worse for the sitter; it isn't Lillo's fault: he's no more to blame than a mirror. Your other painters do the surface—he does the depths; they paint the ripples on the pond, he drags the bottom. He makes flesh seem as fortuitous as clothes. When I look at his portraits of fine ladies in pearls and velvet I seem to see a little naked cowering wisp of a soul sitting beside the big splendid body, like a poor relation in the darkest corner of an opera-box. But look at his pictures of really great people—how great *they* are! There's plenty of ideal there. Take his Professor Clyde; how clearly the man's history is written in those broad steady strokes of the brush: the hard work, the endless patience, the fearless imagination of the great *savant!* Or the picture of Mr. Domfrey—the man who has felt beauty without having the power to create it. The very brush-work expresses the difference between the two; the crowding of nervous tentative lines, the subtler gradations of color, somehow convey a suggestion of dilettantism. You feel what a delicate instrument the man is, how every sense has been tuned to the finest responsiveness." Mrs. Mellish paused, blushing a little at the echo of her own eloquence. "My advice is, don't let George Lillo paint you if you don't want to be found out—or to find yourself out. That's why I've never let him do *me;* I'm waiting for the day of judgment," she ended with a laugh.

Every one but the pretty woman, whose eyes betrayed a quivering impatience to discuss clothes, had listened attentively to Mrs. Mellish. Lillo's presence in New York—he had come over from Paris for the first time in twelve years, to arrange the exhibition of his pictures—gave to the analysis of his methods as personal a flavor as though one had been furtively dissecting his domestic relations. The analogy, indeed, is not unapt; for in Lillo's curiously detached existence it is difficult to figure any closer tie than that which unites him to his pictures. In this light, Mrs. Mellish's flushed harangue seemed not unfitted to the trivialities of the tea hour, and some one almost at once carried on the argument by saying:—"But according to your theory—that the significance of his work depends on the significance of the sitter—his portrait of Vard ought to be a master-piece; and it's his biggest failure."

Alonzo Vard's suicide—he killed himself, strangely enough, the day that Lillo's pictures were first shown—had made his portrait the chief feature of the exhibition. It had been painted ten or twelve years earlier, when the terrible "Boss" was at the height of his power; and if ever man presented a type to stimulate such insight as Lillo's, that man was Vard; yet the portrait was a failure. It was magnificently composed; the technique was dazzling; but the face had been—well, expurgated. It was Vard as Cumberton might have painted him—a common man trying to look at ease in a good coat. The picture had never before been exhibited, and there was a general outcry of disappointment. It wasn't only the critics and the artists who grumbled. Even the big public, which had gaped and shuddered at Vard, revelling in his genial villany, and enjoying in his death that succumbing to divine wrath which, as a spectacle, is next best to its successful defiance—even the public felt itself defrauded. What had the painter done with their hero? Where was the big sneering domineering face that figured so convincingly in political cartoons and patent-medicine advertisements, on cigar-boxes and electioneering posters? They had admired the man for looking his part so boldly; for showing the undisguised blackguard in every line of his coarse body and cruel face; the pseudo-gentleman of Lillo's picture was a poor thing compared to the real Vard. It had been vaguely expected that the great boss's portrait would have the zest of an incriminating document, the scandalous attraction of secret memoirs; and instead, it was as insipid as an obituary. It was as though the artist had been in league with his sitter, had pledged himself to oppose to the lust for post-mortem "revelations" an impassable blank wall of negation. The public was resentful, the critics were aggrieved. Even Mrs. Mellish had to lay down her arms.

"Yes, the portrait of Vard *is* a failure," she admitted, "and I've never known why. If he'd been an obscure elusive type of villain, one could understand Lillo's missing the mark for once; but with that face from the pit—!"

She turned at the announcement of a name which our discussion had drowned, and found herself shaking hands with Lillo.

The pretty woman started and put her hands to her curls; Cumberton dropped a condescending eyelid (he never classed himself by recognizing degrees in the profession), and Mrs. Mellish, cheerfully aware that she had been overheard, said, as she made room for Lillo—

"I wish you'd explain it."

Lillo smoothed his beard and waited for a cup of tea. Then, "Would there be any failures," he said, "if one could explain them?"

"Ah, in some cases I can imagine it's impossible to seize the type—or to say why one has missed it. Some people are like daguerreotypes; in certain lights one can't see them at

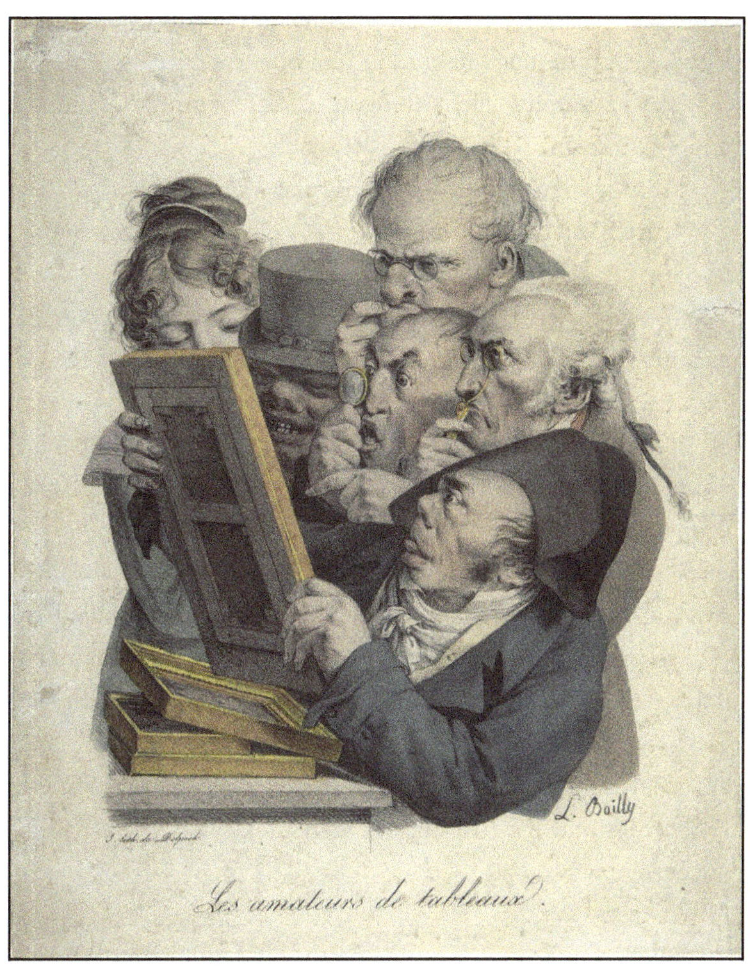

Louis Léopold Boilly, *The Art Connoisseurs*, 1823–28, The Metropolitan Museum of Art, New York, A. Hyatt Mayor Purchase Fund, Marjorie Phelps Starr Bequest, 1989

all. But surely Vard was obvious enough. What I want to know is, what became of him? What did you do with him? How did you manage to shuffle him out of sight?"

"It was much easier than you think. I simply missed an opportunity—"

"That a sign-painter would have seen!"

"Very likely. In fighting shy of the obvious one may miss the significant—"

"—And when I got back from Paris," the pretty woman was heard to wail, "I found all the women here were wearing the very models I'd brought home with me!"

Mrs. Mellish, as became a vigilant hostess, got up and shuffled her guests; and the question of Vard's portrait was dropped.

I left the house with Lillo; and on the way down Fifth Avenue, after one of his long silences, he suddenly asked:

"Is that what is generally said of my picture of Vard? I don't mean in the newspapers, but by the fellows who know?"

I said it was.

He drew a deep breath. "Well," he said, "it's good to know that when one tries to fail one can make such a complete success of it."

"Tries to fail?"

"Well, no; that's not quite it, either; I didn't want to make a failure of Vard's picture, but I did so deliberately, with my eyes open, all the same. It was what one might call a lucid failure."

"But why—?"

"The why of it is rather complicated. I'll tell you some

time—" He hesitated. "Come and dine with me at the club by and by, and I'll tell you afterwards. It's a nice morsel for a psychologist."

At dinner he said little; but I didn't mind that. I had known him for years, and had always found something soothing and companionable in his long abstentions from speech. His silence was never unsocial; it was bland as a natural hush; one felt one's self included in it, not left out. He stroked his beard and gazed absently at me; and when we had finished our coffee and liqueurs we strolled down to his studio.

At the studio—which was less draped, less posed, less consciously "artistic" than those of the smaller men—he handed me a cigar, and fell to smoking before the fire. When he began to talk it was of indifferent matters, and I had dismissed the hope of hearing more of Vard's portrait, when my eye lit on a photograph of the picture. I walked across the room to look at it, and Lillo presently followed with a light.

"It certainly is a complete disguise," he muttered over my shoulder; then he turned away and stooped to a big portfolio propped against the wall.

"Did you ever know Miss Vard?" he asked, with his head in the portfolio; and without waiting for my answer he handed me a crayon sketch of a girl's profile.

I had never seen a crayon of Lillo's, and I lost sight of the sitter's personality in the interest aroused by this new aspect of the master's complex genius. The few lines—faint, yet how decisive!—flowered out of the rough paper with the lightness of opening petals. It was a mere hint of a picture, but vivid as some word that wakens long reverberations in the memory.

I felt Lillo at my shoulder again.

"You knew her, I suppose?"

I had to stop and think. Why, of course I'd known her: a silent handsome girl, showy yet ineffective, whom I had seen without seeing the winter that society had capitulated to Vard. Still looking at the crayon, I tried to trace some connection between the Miss Vard I recalled and the grave young seraph of Lillo's sketch. Had the Vards bewitched him? By what masterstroke of suggestion had he been beguiled into drawing the terrible father as a barber's block, the commonplace daughter as this memorable creature?

"You don't remember much about her? No, I suppose not. She was a quiet girl and nobody noticed her much, even when—" he paused with a smile—"you were all asking Vard to dine."

I winced. Yes, it was true—we had all asked Vard to dine. It was some comfort to think that fate had made him expiate our weakness.

Lillo put the sketch on the mantel-shelf and drew his arm-chair to the fire.

"It's cold tonight. Take another cigar, old man; and some whiskey? There ought to be a bottle and some glasses in that cupboard behind you . . . help yourself . . ."

II

About Vard's portrait? (he began.) Well, I'll tell you. It's a queer story, and most people wouldn't see anything in it. My enemies might say it was a roundabout way of explaining a failure; but you know better than that. Mrs. Mellish was right. Between me and Vard there could be no question of failure. The man was made for me—I felt that the first time I clapped eyes on him. I could hardly keep from asking him to sit to me on the spot; but somehow one couldn't ask favors of the fellow. I sat still and prayed he'd come to me, though; for I was looking for something big for the next Salon. It was twelve years ago—the last time I was out here—and I was ravenous for an opportunity. I had the feeling—do you writer-fellows have it too?—that there was something tremendous in me if it could only be got out; and I felt Vard was the Moses to strike the rock. There were vulgar reasons, too, that made me hunger for a victim. I'd been grinding on obscurely for a good many years, without gold or glory, and the first thing of mine that had made a noise was my picture of Pepita, exhibited the year before. There'd been a lot of talk about that, orders were beginning to come in, and I wanted to follow it up with a rousing big thing at the next Salon. Then the critics had been insinuating that I could do only Spanish things—I suppose I *had* overdone the castanet business; it's a nursery-disease we all go through—and I wanted to show that I had plenty more shot in my locker. Don't you get up every morning meaning to prove you're equal to Balzac or Thackeray? That's the way I felt then; *only give me a chance*, I wanted to shout out to them; and I saw at once that Vard was my chance.

I had come over from Paris in the autumn to paint Mrs. Clingsborough, and I met Vard and his daughter at one of the first dinners I went to. After that I could think of nothing but that man's head. What a type! I raked up all the details of his scandalous history; and there were enough to fill an encyclopedia. The papers were full of him just then; he was mud from head to foot; it was about the time of the big viaduct steal, and irreproachable citizens were forming ineffectual leagues to put him down. And all the time one kept meeting him at dinners—that was the beauty of it! Once I remember seeing him next to the Bishop's wife; I've got a little sketch of that duet somewhere . . . Well, he was simply magnificent, a born ruler; what a splendid condottiere he would have made, in gold armor, with a griffin grinning on his casque! You remember those drawings of Leonardo's, where the knight's face and the outline of his helmet combine in one monstrous saurian profile? He always reminded me of that . . .

But how was I to get at him?—One day it occurred to me to try talking to Miss Vard. She was a monosyllabic person, who didn't seem to see an inch beyond the last remark one had made; but suddenly I found myself blurting out, "I wonder if you know how extraordinarily paintable your father is?" and you should have seen the change that came over her. Her eyes lit up and she looked—well, as I've tried to make her look there. (He glanced up at the sketch.) Yes, she said, *wasn't* her father splendid, and didn't I think him one of the handsomest men I'd ever seen?

That rather staggered me, I confess; I couldn't think her capable of joking on such a subject, yet it seemed impossible that she should be speaking seriously. But she was. I knew it by the way she looked at Vard, who was sitting opposite, his wolfish profile thrown back, the shaggy locks tossed off his narrow high white forehead. The girl worshipped him.

She went on to say how glad she was that I saw him as she did. So many artists admired only regular beauty, the stupid Greek type that was made to be done in marble; but she'd always fancied from what she'd seen of my work—she knew everything I'd done, it appeared—that I looked deeper, cared more for the way in which faces are modelled by temperament and circumstance; "and of course in that sense," she concluded, "my father's face *is* beautiful."

This was even more staggering; but one couldn't question her divine sincerity. I'm afraid my one thought was to take advantage of it; and I let her go on, perceiving that if I wanted to paint Vard all I had to do was to listen.

She poured out her heart. It was a glorious thing for a girl, she said, wasn't it, to be associated with such a life as that? She felt it so strongly, sometimes, that it oppressed her, made her shy and stupid. She was so afraid people would expect her to live up to *him*. But that was absurd, of course; brilliant men so seldom had clever children. Still—did I know?—she would have been happier, much happier, if he hadn't been in public life; if he and she could have hidden themselves away somewhere, with their books and music, and she could have had it all to herself: his cleverness, his learning, his immense unbounded goodness. For no one knew how good he was; no one but herself. Everybody recognized his cleverness, his brilliant abilities; even his enemies had to admit his extraordinary intellectual gifts, and hated him the worse, of course, for the admission; but no one, no one could guess what he was at home. She had heard of great men who were always giving gala performances in public, but whose wives and daughters saw only the empty theater, with the footlights out and the scenery stacked in the wings; but with him it was just the other way: wonderful as he was in public, in society, she sometimes felt he wasn't doing himself justice—he was so much more wonderful at home. It was like carrying a guilty secret about with her: his friends, his admirers, would never forgive her if they found out that he kept all his best things for *her!*

I don't quite know what I felt in listening to her. I was chiefly taken up with leading her on to the point I had in view; but even through my personal preoccupation I remember being struck by the fact that, though she talked foolishly, she didn't talk like a fool. She was not stupid; she was not obtuse; one felt that her impassive surface was alive with delicate points of perception; and this fact, coupled with her crystalline frankness, flung me back on a startled revision of my impressions of her father. He came out of the test more monstrous than ever, as an ugly image reflected in clear water is made uglier by the purity of the medium. Even then I felt a pang at the use to which fate had put the mountain-pool of Miss Vard's spirit, and an uneasy sense that my own reflection there was not one to linger over. It was odd that I should have scrupled to deceive, on one small point, a girl already so hugely cheated; perhaps it was the completeness of her delusion that gave it the sanctity of a religious belief. At any rate, a distinct sense of discomfort tempered the satisfaction with which, a day or two later, I heard from her that her father had consented to give me a few sittings.

I'm afraid my scruples vanished when I got him before my easel. He was immense, and he was unexplored. From my point of view he'd never been done before—I was his Cortez. As he talked the wonder grew. His daughter came with him, and I began to think she was right in saying that he kept his best for her. It wasn't that she drew him out, or guided the conversation; but one had a sense of delicate vigilance, hardly more perceptible than one of those atmospheric influences that give the pulses a happier turn. She was a vivifying climate. I had meant to turn the talk to public affairs, but it slipped toward books and art, and I was faintly aware of its being kept there without undue pressure. Before long I saw the value of the diversion. It was easy enough to get at the political Vard: the other aspect was rarer and more instructive. His daughter had described him as a scholar. He wasn't that, of course, in any intrinsic sense: like most men of his type he had gulped his knowledge standing, as he had snatched his food from lunch-counters; the wonder of it lay in his extraordinary power of assimilation. It was the strangest instance of a mind to which erudition had given force and fluency without culture; his learning had not educated his perceptions: it was an implement serving to slash others rather than to polish himself. I have said that at first sight he was immense; but as I studied him he began to lessen under my scrutiny. His depth was a false perspective painted on a wall.

It was there that my difficulty lay: I had prepared too big a canvas for him. Intellectually his scope was considerable, but it was like the digital reach of a mediocre pianist—it didn't make him a great musician. And morally he wasn't bad enough; his corruption wasn't sufficiently imaginative to be interesting. It was not so much a means to an end as a kind of virtuosity practiced for its own sake, like a highly-developed skill in cannoning billiard balls. After all, the point of view is what gives distinction to either vice or virtue: a morality with ground-glass windows is no duller than a narrow cynicism.

His daughter's presence—she always came with him—gave unintentional emphasis to these conclusions; for where she was richest he was naked. She had a deep-rooted delicacy that drew color and perfume from the very center of her being: his sentiments, good or bad, were as detachable as his cuffs. Thus her nearness, planned, as I guessed, with the tender intention of displaying, elucidating him, of making him accessible in detail to my dazzled perceptions—this pious design in fact defeated itself. She made him appear at his best, but she cheapened that best by her proximity. For the man was vulgar to the core; vulgar in spite of his force and magnitude; thin, hollow, spectacular; a lath-and-plaster bogey—

Did she suspect it? I think not—then. He was wrapped in her impervious faith . . . The papers? Oh, their charges were set down to political rivalry; and the only people she saw were his hangers-on, or the fashionable set who had taken him up for their amusement. Besides, she would never have found out in that way: at a direct accusation her resentment would have flamed up and smothered her judgment. If the truth came to her, it would come through knowing intimately some one—different; through—how shall I put it?—an imperceptible shifting of her center of gravity. My besetting fear was that I couldn't count on her obtuseness. She wasn't what is called clever; she left that to him; but she was exquisitely good; and now and then she had intuitive felicities that frightened me. Do I make you see her? We fellows can explain better with the brush; I don't know how to mix my words or lay them on. She wasn't clever; but her heart thought—that's all I can say . . .

If she'd been stupid it would have been easy enough: I could have painted him as he was. Could have? I did—brushed the face in one day from memory; it was the very man! I painted it out before she came: I couldn't bear to have her see it. I had the feeling that I held her faith in him in my hands, carrying it like a brittle object through a jostling mob; a hair's-breadth swerve and it was in splinters.

When she wasn't there I tried to reason myself out of these subtleties. My business was to paint Vard as he was—if his daughter didn't mind his looks, why should I? The opportunity was magnificent—I knew that by the way his face had leapt out of the canvas at my first touch. It would have been a big thing. Before every sitting I swore to myself I'd do it; then she came, and sat near him, and I—didn't.

I knew that before long she'd notice I was shirking the face. Vard himself took little interest in the portrait, but she watched me closely, and one day when the sitting was over she stayed behind and asked me when I meant to begin what she called "the likeness." I guessed from her tone that the embarrassment was all on my side, or that if she felt any it was at having to touch a vulnerable point in my pride. Thus far the only doubt that troubled her was a distrust of my ability. Well, I put her off with any rot you please: told her she must trust me, must let me wait for the inspiration; that some day the face would come; I should see it suddenly—feel it under my brush . . . The poor child believed me: you can make a woman believe almost anything she doesn't quite understand. She was abashed at her philistinism, and begged me not to tell her father—he would make such fun of her!

After that—well, the sittings went on. Not many, of course; Vard was too busy to give me much time. Still, I could have done him ten times over. Never had I found my formula with such ease, such assurance; there were no hesitations, no obstructions—the face was *there*, waiting for me; at times it almost shaped itself on the canvas. Unfortunately Miss Vard was there too . . .

All this time the papers were busy with the viaduct scandal. The outcry was getting louder. You remember the circumstances? One of Vard's associates—Bardwell, wasn't it?—threatened disclosures. The rival machine got hold of him, the Independents took him to their bosom, and the press shrieked for an investigation. It was not the first storm Vard had weathered, and his face wore just the right shade of cool vigilance; he wasn't the man to fall into the mistake of appearing too easy. His demeanor would have been superb if it had been inspired by a sense of his own strength; but it struck me rather as based on contempt for his antagonists.

Success is an inverted telescope through which one's enemies are apt to look too small and too remote. As for Miss Vard, her serenity was undiminished; but I half-detected a defiance in her unruffled sweetness, and during the last sittings I had the factitious vivacity of a hostess who hears her best china crashing.

One day it *did* crash: the headlines of the morning papers shouted the catastrophe at me:—"The Monster forced to disgorge—Warrant out against Vard—Bardwell the Boss's Boomerang"—you know the kind of thing.

When I had read the papers I threw them down and went out. As it happened, Vard was to have given me a sitting that morning; but there would have been a certain irony in waiting for him. I wished I had finished the picture—I wished I'd never thought of painting it. I wanted to shake off the whole business, to put it out of my mind, if I could: I had the feeling—I don't know if I can describe it—that there was a kind of disloyalty to the poor girl in my even acknowledging to myself that I knew what all the papers were howling from the housetops . . .

I had walked for an hour when it suddenly occurred to me that Miss Vard might, after all, come to the studio at the appointed hour. Why should she? I could conceive of no reason; but the mere thought of what, if she *did* come, my absence would imply to her, sent me bolting back to Twelfth Street. It was a presentiment, if you like, for she was there.

As she rose to meet me a newspaper slipped from her hand: I'd been fool enough, when I went out, to leave the damned things lying all over the place.

I muttered some apology for being late, and she said reassuringly:

"But my father's not here yet."

"Your father—?" I could have kicked myself for the way I bungled it!

"He went out very early this morning, and left word that he would meet me here at the usual hour."

She faced me, with an eye full of bright courage, across the newspaper lying between us.

"He ought to be here in a moment now—he's always so punctual. But my watch is a little fast, I think."

She held it out to me almost gaily, and I was just pretending to compare it with mine, when there was a smart rap on the door and Vard stalked in. There was always a civic majesty in his gait, an air of having just stepped off his pedestal and of dissembling an oration in his umbrella; and that day he surpassed himself. Miss Vard had turned pale at the knock; but the mere sight of him replenished her veins, and if she now avoided my eye, it was in mere pity for my discomfiture.

I was in fact the only one of the three who didn't instantly "play up"; but such virtuosity was inspiring, and by the time Vard had thrown off his coat and dropped into a senatorial pose, I was ready to pitch into my work. I swore I'd do his face then and there; do it as she saw it; she sat close to him, and I had only to glance at her while I painted—

Vard himself was masterly: his talk rattled through my hesitations and embarrassments like a brisk northwester sweeping the dry leaves from its path. Even his daughter showed the sudden brilliance of a lamp from which the shade has been removed. We were all surprisingly vivid—it felt, somehow, as though we were being photographed by flash-light . . .

It was the best sitting we'd ever had—but unfortunately it didn't last more than ten minutes.

It was Vard's secretary who interrupted us—a slinking chap called Cornley, who burst in, as white as sweetbread, with the face of a depositor who hears his bank has stopped payment. Miss Vard started up as he entered, but caught herself together and dropped back into her chair. Vard, who had taken out a cigarette, held the tip tranquilly to his fusee.

"You're here, thank God!" Cornley cried. "There's no time to be lost, Mr. Vard. I've got a carriage waiting round the corner in Thirteenth Street—"

Vard looked at the tip of his cigarette.

"A carriage in Thirteenth Street? My good fellow, my own brougham is at the door."

"I know, I know—but *they*'re there too, sir; or they will be, inside of a minute. For God's sake, Mr. Vard, don't trifle!—There's a way out by Thirteenth Street, I tell you"—

"Bardwell's myrmidons, eh?" said Vard. "Help me on with my overcoat, Cornley, will you?"

Cornley's teeth chattered.

"Mr. Vard, your best friends . . . Miss Vard, won't you speak to your father?" He turned to me haggardly;—"We can get out by the back way?"

I nodded.

Vard stood towering—in some infernal way he seemed

literally to rise to the situation—one hand in the bosom of his coat, in the attitude of patriotism in bronze. I glanced at his daughter: she hung on him with a drowning look. Suddenly she straightened herself; there was something of Vard in the way she faced her fears—a kind of primitive calm we drawing-room folk don't have. She stepped to him and laid her hand on his arm. The pause hadn't lasted ten seconds.

"Father—" she said.

Vard threw back his head and swept the studio with a sovereign eye.

"The back way, Mr. Vard, the back way," Cornley whimpered. "For God's sake, sir, don't lose a minute."

Vard transfixed his abject henchman.

"I have never yet taken the back way," he enunciated; and, with a gesture matching the words, he turned to me and bowed.

"I regret the disturbance"—and he walked to the door. His daughter was at his side, alert, transfigured.

"Stay here, my dear."

"Never!"

They measured each other an instant; then he drew her arm in his. She flung back one look at me—a pæan of victory—and they passed out with Cornley at their heels.

I wish I'd finished the face then; I believe I could have caught something of the look she had tried to make me see in him. Unluckily I was too excited to work that day or the next, and within the week the whole business came out. If the indictment wasn't a put-up job—and on that I believe there were two opinions—all that followed was. You remember the farcical trial, the packed jury, the compliant judge, the triumphant acquittal? . . . It's a spectacle that always carries conviction to the voter: Vard was never more popular than after his "exoneration" . . .

I didn't see Miss Vard for weeks. It was she who came to me at length; came to the studio alone, one afternoon at dusk. She had—what shall I say?—a veiled manner; as though she had dropped a fine gauze between us. I waited for her to speak.

She glanced about the room, admiring a hawthorn vase I had picked up at auction. Then, after a pause, she said:

"You haven't finished the picture?"

"Not quite," I said.

She asked to see it, and I wheeled out the easel and threw the drapery back.

"Oh," she murmured, "you haven't gone on with the face?"

I shook my head.

She looked down on her clasped hands and up at the picture; not once at me.

"You—you're going to finish it?"

"Of course," I cried, throwing the revived purpose into my voice. By God, I would finish it!

The merest tinge of relief stole over her face, faint as the first thin chirp before daylight.

"Is it so very difficult?" she asked tentatively.

"Not insuperably, I hope."

She sat silent, her eyes on the picture. At length, with an effort, she brought out: "Shall you want more sittings?"

For a second I blundered between two conflicting conjectures; then the truth came to me with a leap, and I cried out, "No, no more sittings!"

She looked up at me then for the first time; looked too soon, poor child; for in the spreading light of reassurance that made her eyes like a rainy dawn, I saw, with terrible distinctness, the rout of her disbanded hopes. I knew that she knew . . .

I finished the picture and sent it home within a week. I tried to make it—what you see.—Too late, you say? Yes—for her; but not for me or for the public. If she could be made to feel, for a day longer, for an hour even, that her miserable secret *was* a secret—why, she'd made it seem worth while to me to chuck my own ambitions for that . . .

Lillo rose, and taking down the sketch stood looking at it in silence.

After a while I ventured, "And Miss Vard—?"

He opened the portfolio and put the sketch back, tying the strings with deliberation. Then, turning to relight his cigar at the lamp, he said: "She died last year, thank God."

A Landscape Painter

Henry James

Published in A Landscape Painter *by Scott and Seltzer, 1914; originally appeared in* The Atlantic Monthly, *February 1866.*

Do you remember how, a dozen years ago, a number of our friends were startled by the report of the rupture of young Locksley's engagement with Miss Leary? This event made some noise in its day. Both parties possessed certain claims to distinction: Locksley in his wealth, which was believed to be enormous, and the young lady in her beauty, which was in truth very great. I used to hear that her lover was fond of comparing her to the Venus of Milo; and, indeed, if you can imagine the mutilated goddess with her full complement of limbs, dressed out by Madame de Crinoline, and engaged in small talk beneath the drawing-room chandelier, you may obtain a vague notion of Miss Josephine Leary. Locksley, you remember, was rather a short man, dark, and not particularly good-looking; and when he walked about with his betrothed, it was half a matter of surprise that he should have ventured to propose to a young lady of such heroic proportions. Miss Leary had the gray eyes and auburn hair which I have always assigned to the famous statue. The one defect in her face, in spite of an expression of great candor and sweetness, was a certain lack of animation. What it was besides her beauty that attracted Locksley I never discovered: perhaps, since his attachment was so short-lived, it was her beauty alone. I say that his attachment was of brief duration, because the rupture was understood to have come from him. Both he and Miss Leary very wisely held their tongues on the matter; but among their friends and enemies it of course received a hundred explanations. That most popular with Locksley's well-wishers was that he had backed out (these events are discussed, you know, in fashionable circles very much as an expected prizefight which has miscarried is canvassed in reunions of another kind) only on flagrant evidence of the lady's—what, faithlessness?—on overwhelming proof of the most *mercenary* spirit on the part of Miss Leary. You see, our friend was held capable of doing battle for an "idea." It must be owned that this was a novel charge; but, for myself, having long known Mrs. Leary, the mother, who was a widow with four daughters, to be an inveterate old screw, I took the liberty of accrediting the existence of a similar propensity in her eldest born. I suppose that the young lady's family had, on their own side, a very plausible version of their disappointment. It was, however, soon made up to them by Josephine's marriage with a gentleman of expectations very nearly as brilliant as those of her old suitor. And what was *his* compensation? That is precisely my story.

Locksley disappeared, as you will remember, from public view. The events above alluded to happened in March. On calling at his lodgings in April, I was told he had gone to the "country." But towards the last of May I met him. He told me that he was on the look-out for a quiet, unfrequented place on the seashore, where he might rusticate and sketch. He was looking very poorly. I suggested Newport, and I remember he hardly had the energy to smile at the simple joke. We parted without my having been able to satisfy him, and for a very long time I quite lost sight of him. He died seven years ago, at the age of thirty-five. For five years, accordingly, he managed to shield his life from the eyes of men. Through circumstances which I need not detail, a large portion of his personal property has come into my hands. You will remember that he was a man of what are called elegant tastes: that is, he was seriously interested in arts and letters. He wrote some very bad poetry, but he produced a number of remarkable paintings. He left a mass of papers on all subjects, few of which are adapted to be generally interesting. A portion of them, however, I highly prize,—that which constitutes his private diary. It extends from his twenty-fifth to his thirtieth year, at which period it breaks off suddenly. If you will come to my house, I will show you such of his pictures and sketches as I possess, and, I trust, convert you to my opinion that he had in him the stuff of a great painter. Meanwhile I will place before you the last hundred pages of his diary, as an answer to your inquiry regarding the ultimate view taken by the great Nemesis of his treatment of Miss Leary,—his scorn of the magnificent Venus Victrix. The recent decease of the one person who had a voice paramount to mine in the disposal of Locksley's effects enables me to act without reserve.

Cragthrope, June 9th.—I have been sitting some minutes, pen in hand, pondering whether on this new earth, beneath this new sky, I had better resume these occasional records of my idleness. I think I will at all events make the experiment. If we fail, as Lady Macbeth remarks, we fail. I find my entries have been longest when my life has been dullest. I doubt not, therefore, that, once launched into the monotony of village life, I shall sit scribbling from morning till night. If nothing happens— But my prophetic soul tells me that something *will* happen. I am determined that something shall,—if it be nothing else than that I paint a picture.

When I came up to bed half an hour ago, I was deadly sleepy. Now, after looking out of the window a little while, my brain is strong and clear, and I feel as if I could write till morning. But, unfortunately, I have nothing to write about. And then, if I expect to rise early, I must turn in betimes. The whole village is asleep, godless metropolitan that I am! The lamps on the square without flicker in the wind; there is nothing abroad but the blue darkness and the smell of the rising tide. I have spent the whole day on my legs, trudging from one side of the peninsula to the other. What a trump is old Mrs. M——, to have thought of this place! I must write her a letter of passionate thanks. Never before, it seems to me, have I known pure coast-scenery. Never before have I relished the beauties of wave, rock, and cloud. I am filled with a sensuous ecstasy at the unparalleled life, light, and transparency of the air. I am stricken mute with reverent admiration at the stupendous resources possessed by the ocean in the way of color and sound; and as yet, I suppose,

I have not seen half of them. I came in to supper hungry, weary, footsore, sunburnt, dirty,—happier, in short, than I have been for a twelvemonth. And now for the victories of the brush!

June 11th.—Another day afoot and also afloat. I resolved this morning to leave this abominable little tavern. I can't stand my feather-bed another night. I determined to find some other prospect than the town-pump and the "drug-store." I questioned my host, after breakfast, as to the possibility of getting lodgings in any of the outlying farms and cottages. But my host either did not or would not know anything about the matter. So I resolved to wander forth and seek my fortune,—to roam inquisitive through the neighborhood, and appeal to the indigenous sentiment of hospitality. But never did I see a folk so devoid of this amiable quality. By dinner-time I had given up in despair. After dinner I strolled down to the harbor, which is close at hand. The brightness and breeziness of the water tempted me to hire a boat and resume my explorations. I procured an old tub, with a short stump of a mast, which, being planted quite in the center, gave the craft much the appearance of an inverted mushroom. I made for what I took to be, and what is, an island, lying long and low, some three or four miles, over against the town. I sailed for half an hour directly before the wind, and at last found myself aground on the shelving beach of a quiet little cove. *Such* a little cove! So bright, so still, so warm, so remote from the town, which lay off in the distance, white and semicircular! I leaped ashore, and dropped my anchor. Before me rose a steep cliff, crowned with an old ruined fort or tower. I made my way up, and about to the landward entrance. The fort is a hollow old shell. Looking upward from the beach, you see the harmless blue sky through the gaping loopholes. Its interior is choked with rocks and brambles, and masses of fallen masonry. I scrambled up to the parapet, and obtained a noble sea-view. Beyond the broad bay I saw miniature town and country mapped out before me; and on the other hand, I saw the infinite Atlantic,—over which, by the by, all the pretty things are brought from Paris. I spent the whole afternoon in wandering hither and thither over the hills that encircle the little cove in which I had landed, heedless of the minutes and my steps, watching the sailing clouds and the cloudy sails on the horizon, listening to the musical attrition of the tidal pebbles, killing innocuous suckers. The only particular sensation I remember was that of being ten years old again, together with a general impression of Saturday afternoon, of the liberty to go in wading or even swimming, and of the prospect of limping home in the dusk with a wondrous story of having *almost* caught a turtle. When I returned, I found—but I know very well what I found, and I need hardly repeat it here for my mortification. Heaven knows I never was a practical character. What thought I about the tide? There lay the old tub, high and dry, with the rusty anchor protruding from the flat green stones and the shallow puddles left by the receding wave. Moving the boat an inch, much more a dozen yards, was quite beyond my strength. I slowly reascended the cliff, to see if from its summit any help was discernible. None was within sight; and I was about to go down again in

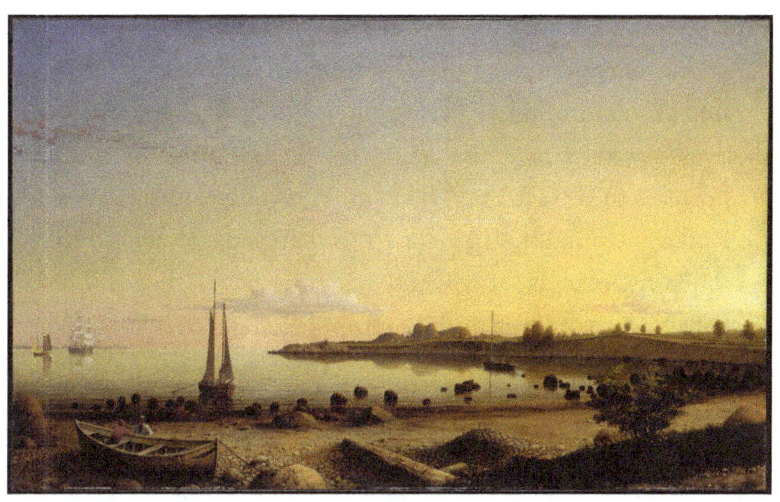

Fitz Henry Lane (formerly Fitz Hugh Lane), *Stage Fort Across Gloucester Harbor*, 1862, The Metropolitan Museum of Art, New York, Purchase, Rogers and Fletcher Funds, Erving and Joyce Wolf Fund, Raymond J. Horowitz Gift, Bequest of Richard De Wolfe Brixey, by exchange, and John Osgood and Elizabeth Amis Cameron Blanchard Memorial Fund, 1978 profound dejection, when I saw a trim little sailboat shoot out from behind a neighboring bluff, and advance along the shore. I quickened pace. On reaching the beach, I found the newcomer standing out about a hundred yards. The man at the helm appeared to regard me with some interest. With a mute prayer that his feeling might be akin to compassion, I invited him by voice and gesture to make for a little point of rocks a short distance above us, where I proceeded to join him. I told him my story, and he readily took me aboard. He was a civil old gentleman, of the seafaring sort, who appeared to be cruising about in the evening breeze for his pleasure. On landing, I visited the proprietor of my old tub, related my misadventure, and offered to pay damages, if the boat should turn out in the morning to have sustained any. Meanwhile, I suppose, it is held secure against the next tidal revolution, however insidious.—But for my old gentleman. I have decidedly picked up an acquaintance, if not made a friend. I gave him a very good cigar; and before we reached home, we had become thoroughly intimate. In exchange for my cigar, he gave me his name; and there was that in his tone which seemed to imply that I had by no means the worst of the bargain. His name is Richard Blunt, "though most people," he added, "call me Captain, for short." He then proceeded to inquire my own titles and pretensions. I told him no lies, but I told him only half the truth; and if he chooses to indulge mentally in any romantic understatements, why, he is welcome, and bless his simple heart! The fact is, that I have broken with the past. I have decided, coolly and calmly, as I believe, that it is necessary to my success, or, at any rate, to my happiness, to abjure for a while my conventional self, and to assume a simple, natural character. How can a man be simple and natural who is known to have a hundred thousand a year? That is the supreme curse. It's bad enough to have it: to be known to have it, to be known only because you have it, is most damnable. I suppose I am too proud to be successfully rich. Let me see how poverty will serve my turn. I have taken a fresh start. I have determined to stand upon my own merits. If they fail me, I shall fall back upon my millions; but with God's help I will test them, and see what kind of stuff I am made of. To be young, to be strong, to be poor,—such, in this blessed nineteenth century, is the great basis of solid success. I have resolved to take at least one brief draught from the pure founts of inspiration of my time. I replied to the Captain with such reservations as a brief survey of these principles dictated. What a luxury to pass in a poor man's mind for his brother! I begin to respect myself. Thus much the Captain knows: that I am an educated man, with a taste for painting; that I have come hither for the purpose of cultivating this taste by the study of coast scenery, and for my health. I have reason to believe, moreover, that he suspects me of limited means and of being a good deal of an economist. Amen! *Vogue la galère!* But the point of my story is in his very hospitable offer of lodgings. I had been telling him of my ill success of the morning in the pursuit of the same. He is an odd union of the gentleman of the old school and the old-fashioned, hot-headed merchant-captain. I suppose that certain traits in these characters are readily convertible.

"Young man," said he, after taking several meditative

puffs of his cigar, "I don't see the point of your living in a tavern, when there are folks about you with more house-room than they know what to do with. A tavern is only half a house, just as one of these new-fashioned screw-propellers is only half a ship. Suppose you walk round and take a look at my place. I own quite a respectable house over yonder to the left of the town. Do you see that old wharf with the tumble-down warehouses, and the long row of elms behind it? I live right in the midst of the elms. We have the dearest little garden in the world, stretching down to the water's edge. It's all as quiet as anything can be, short of a graveyard. The back windows, you know, overlook the harbor; and you can see twenty miles up the bay, and fifty miles out to sea. You can paint to yourself there the livelong day, with no more fear of intrusion than if you were out yonder at the light-ship. There's no one but myself and my daughter, who's a perfect lady, Sir. She teaches music in a young ladies' school. You see, money's an object, as they say. We have never taken boarders yet, because none came in our track; but I guess we can learn the ways. I suppose you've boarded before; you can put us up to a thing or two."

There was something so kindly and honest in the old man's weather-beaten face, something so friendly in his address, that I forthwith struck a bargain with him, subject to his daughter's approval. I am to have her answer to-morrow. This same daughter strikes me as rather a dark spot in the picture. Teacher in a young ladies' school,—probably the establishment of which Mrs. M—— spoke to me. I suppose she's over thirty. I think I know the species.

June 12th, A.M.—I have really nothing to do but to scribble. "Barkis is willing." Captain Blunt brought me word this morning that his daughter smiles propitious. I am to report this evening; but I shall send my slender baggage in an hour or two.

P. M.—Here I am, housed. The house is less than a mile from the inn, and reached by a very pleasant road, skirting the harbor. At about six o'clock I presented myself. Captain Blunt had described the place. A very civil old negress admitted me, and ushered me into the garden, where I found my friends watering their flowers. The old man was in his house-coat and slippers. He gave me a cordial welcome. There is something delightfully easy in his manners,—and in Miss Blunt's, too, for that matter. She received me very nicely. The late Mrs. Blunt was probably a well-bred woman. As for Miss Blunt's being thirty, she is about twenty-four. She wore a fresh white dress, with a violet ribbon at her neck, and a rosebud in her button-hole,—or whatever corresponds thereto on the feminine bosom. I thought I discerned in this costume a vague intention of courtesy, of deference, of celebrating my arrival. I don't believe Miss Blunt wears white muslin every day. She shook hands with me, and made me a very frank little speech about her hospitality. "We have never had any inmates before," said she; "and we are, consequently, new to the business. I don't know what you expect. I hope you don't expect a great deal. You must ask for anything you want. If we can give it, we shall be very glad to do so; if we can't, I give you warning that we shall refuse outright." Bravo, Miss Blunt! The best of it is, that she is decidedly beautiful,—and in the grand manner: tall, and rather plump. What is the orthodox description of a pretty girl?—white and red? Miss Blunt is not a pretty girl, she is a handsome woman. She leaves an impression of black and red; that is, she is a florid brunette. She has a great deal of wavy black hair, which encircles her head like a dusky glory, a smoky halo. Her eyebrows, too, are black, but her eyes themselves are of a rich blue gray, the color of those slate-cliffs which I saw yesterday, weltering under the tide. Her mouth, however, is her strong point. It is very large, and contains the finest row of teeth in all this weary world. Her smile is eminently intelligent. Her chin is full, and somewhat heavy. All this is a tolerable catalogue, but no picture. I have been tormenting my brain to discover whether it was her coloring or her form that impressed me most. Fruitless speculation! Seriously, I think it was neither; it was her movement. She walks a queen. It was the conscious poise of her head, the unconscious "hang" of her arms, the careless grace and dignity with which she lingered along the garden-path, smelling a red red rose! She has very little to say, apparently; but when she speaks, it is to the point, and if the point suggests it, with a very sweet smile. Indeed, if she is not talkative, it is not from timidity. Is it from indifference? Time will elucidate this, as well as other matters. I cling to the hypothesis that she is amiable. She is, moreover, intelligent; she is probably quite reserved; and she is possibly very proud. She is, in short, a woman of character. There you are, Miss Blunt, at full length,—emphatically the portrait of a lady. After tea, she gave us some music in the parlor. I confess that I was more taken with the picture of the dusky little room, lighted by the single candle on the piano, and by the *effect* of Miss Blunt's performance, than with its meaning. She appears to possess a very brilliant touch.

June 18th.—I have now been here almost a week. I occupy two very pleasant rooms. My painting-room is a vast and rather bare apartment, with a very good southern light. I have decked it out with a few old prints and sketches, and have already grown very fond of it. When I had disposed my artistic odds and ends in as picturesque a fashion as possible, I called in my hosts. The Captain looked about silently for some moments, and then inquired hopefully if I had ever tried my hand at a ship. On learning that I had not yet got to ships, he relapsed into a deferential silence. His daughter smiled and questioned very graciously, and called everything beautiful and delightful; which rather disappointed me, as I had taken her to be a woman of some originality. She is rather a puzzle;—or is she, indeed, a very commonplace person, and the fault in me, who am forever taking women to mean a great deal more than their Maker intended? Regarding Miss Blunt I have collected a few facts. She is not twenty-four, but twenty-seven years old. She has taught music ever since she was twenty, in a large boarding-school just out of the town, where she originally got her education. Her salary in this establishment, which is, I believe, a tolerably flourishing one, and the proceeds of a few additional lessons, constitute the chief revenues of the household. But Blunt fortunately owns his house, and his needs and habits are of the simplest kind. What does he or his daughter know of the great worldly theory of necessities, the great worldly scale of pleasures? Miss Blunt's only luxuries are a subscription to the circulating library, and an occasional walk on the beach, which, like one of Miss Brontë's heroines, she paces in company with an old Newfoundland dog. I am afraid she is sadly ignorant. She reads nothing but novels. I am bound to believe, however, that she has derived from the perusal of these works a certain practical science of her own. "I read all the novels I can get," she said yesterday; "but I only like the good ones. I do so like Zanoni, which I have just finished." I must set her to work at some of the masters. I should like some of those fretful New-York heiresses to see how this woman lives. I wish, too, that half a dozen of *ces messieurs* of the clubs might take a peep at the present way of life of their humble servant. We breakfast at eight o'clock. Immediately afterwards, Miss Blunt, in a shabby old bonnet and shawl, starts off to school. If the weather is fine, the Captain goes out a-fishing, and I am left to my own devices. Twice I have accompanied the old man. The second time I was lucky enough to catch a big bluefish, which we had for dinner. The Captain is an excellent specimen of the sturdy navigator, with his loose blue clothes, his ultra-divergent legs, his crisp white hair, and his jolly thick-skinned visage. He comes of a sea-faring English race. There is more or less of the ship's cabin in the general aspect of this antiquated house. I have heard the winds whistle about its walls, on two or three occasions, in true mid-ocean style. And then the illusion is heightened, somehow or other, by the extraordinary intensity of the light. My painting-room is a grand observatory of the clouds. I sit by the half-hour, watching them sail past my high, uncurtained windows. At the back part of the room, something tells you that they belong to an ocean sky; and there, in truth, as you draw nearer, you behold the vast, gray complement of sea. This quarter of the town is perfectly quiet. Human activity seems to have passed over it, never again to return, and to have left a kind of deposit of melancholy resignation. The streets are clean, bright, and airy; but this fact seems only to add to the intense sobriety. It implies that the unobstructed heavens are in the secret of their decline. There is something ghostly in the perpetual stillness. We frequently hear the rattling of the yards and the issuing of orders on the barks and schooners anchored out in the harbor.

June 28th.—My experiment works far better than I had hoped. I am thoroughly at my ease; my peace of mind quite passeth understanding. I work diligently; I have none but pleasant thoughts. The past has almost lost its terrors. For a week now I have been out sketching daily. The Captain carries me to a certain point on the shore of the harbor, I disembark and strike across the fields to a spot where I have established a kind of *rendezvous* with a particular effect of rock and shadow, which has been tolerably faithful to its appointment. Here I set up my easel, and paint till sunset. Then I retrace my steps and meet the boat. I am in every way much encouraged. The horizon of my work grows perceptibly wider. And then I am inexpressibly happy in the conviction that I am not wholly unfit for a life of (moderate) labor and (comparative) privation. I am quite in love with my poverty, if I may call it so. As why should I not? At this rate I don't spend eight hundred a year.

July 12th.—We have been having a week of bad weather: constant rain, night and day. This is certainly at once the brightest and the blackest spot in New England. The skies can smile, assuredly; but how they can frown! I have been painting rather languidly, and at a great disadvantage, at my window. . . . Through all this pouring and pattering, Miss Blunt sallies forth to her pupils. She envelops her beautiful head in a great woollen hood, her beautiful figure in a kind of feminine mackintosh; her feet she puts into heavy clogs, and over the whole she balances a cotton umbrella. When she comes home, with the rain-drops glistening on her red cheeks and her dark lashes, her cloak bespattered with mud, and her hands red with the cool damp, she is a profoundly wholesome spectacle. I never fail to make her a very low bow, for which she repays me with an extraordinary smile. This working-day side of her character is what especially pleases me in Miss Blunt. This holy working-dress of loveliness and dignity sits upon her with the simplicity of an antique drapery. Little use has she for whalebones and furbelows. What a poetry there is, after all, in red hands! I kiss yours, Mademoiselle. I do so because you are self-helpful; because you earn your living; because you are honest, simple, and ignorant (for a sensible woman, that is); because you speak and act to the point; because, in short, you are so unlike—certain of your sisters.

July 16th.—On Monday it cleared up generously. When I went to my window, on rising, I found sky and sea looking, for their brightness and freshness, like a clever English water-color. The ocean is of a deep purple blue; above it, the pure, bright sky looks pale, though it bends with an infinite depth over the inland horizon. Here and there on the dark breezy water gleams the white cap of a wave, or flaps the white cloak of a fishing-boat. I have been sketching sedulously; I have discovered, within a couple of miles' walk, a large, lonely pond, set in quite a grand landscape of barren rocks and grassy slopes. At one extremity is a broad outlook on the open sea; at the other, deep buried in the foliage of an apple-orchard, stands an old haunted-looking farmhouse. To the west of the pond is a wide expanse of rock and grass, of beach and marsh. The sheep browse over it as upon a Highland moor. Except a few stunted firs and cedars, there is not a tree in sight. When I want shade, I seek it in the shelter of one of the great mossy boulders which upheave their scintillating shoulders to the sun, or of the long shallow dells where a tangle of blackberry-bushes hedges about a sky-reflecting pool. I have encamped over against a plain, brown hillside, which, with laborious patience, I am transferring to canvas; and as we have now had the same clear sky for several days, I have almost finished quite a satisfactory little study. I go forth immediately after breakfast. Miss Blunt furnishes me with a napkin full of bread and cold meat, which at the noonday hour, in my sunny solitude, within sight of the slumbering ocean, I voraciously convey to my lips with my discolored fingers. At seven o'clock I return to tea, at which repast we each tell the story of our day's work. For poor Miss Blunt, it is day after day the same story: a wearisome round of visits to the school, and to the houses of the mayor, the parson, the butcher, the baker, whose young ladies, of course, all receive instruction on the piano. But she doesn't complain, nor, indeed, does she look very weary. When she has put on a fresh calico dress for tea, and arranged her hair anew, and with these improvements flits about with that quiet hither and thither of her gentle footsteps, preparing our evening meal, peeping into the teapot, cutting the solid loaf,—or when, sitting down on the low door-step, she reads out select scraps from the evening paper,—or else, when, tea being over, she folds her arms, (an attitude which becomes her mightily,) and, still sitting on the door-step, gossips away the evening in comfortable idleness, while her father and I indulge in the fragrant pipe, and watch the lights shining out, one by one, in different quarters of the darkling bay: at these moments she is as pretty, as cheerful, as careless as it becomes a sensible woman to be. What a pride the Captain takes in his daughter! And she, in return, how perfect is her devotion to the old man! He is proud of her grace, of her tact, of her good sense, of her wit, such as it is. He thinks her to be the most accomplished of women. He waits upon her as if, instead of his old familiar Esther, she were a newly inducted daughter-in-law. And indeed, if I were his own son, he could not be kinder to me. They are certainly—nay, why should I not say it?—*we* are certainly a very happy little household. Will it last forever? I say *we*, because both father and daughter have given me a hundred assurances—he direct, and she, if I don't flatter myself, after the manner of her sex, indirect—that I am already a valued friend. It is natural enough that I should have gained their good-will. They have received at my hands inveterate courtesy. The way to the old man's heart is through a studied consideration of his daughter. He knows, I imagine, that I admire Miss Blunt. But if I should at any time fall below the mark of ceremony, I should have an account to settle with him. All this is as it should be. When people have to economize with the dollars and cents, they have a right to be splendid in their feelings. I have prided myself not a little on my good manners towards my hostess. That my bearing has been without reproach is, however, a fact which I do not, in any degree, set down here to my credit; for I would defy the most impertinent of men (whoever he is) to forget himself with this young lady, without leave unmistakably given. Those deep, dark eyes have a strong prohibitory force. I record the circumstance simply because in future years, when my charming friend shall have become a distant shadow, it will be pleasant, in turning over these pages, to find written testimony to a number of points which I shall be apt to charge solely upon my imagination. I wonder whether Miss Blunt, in days to come, referring to the tables of her memory for some trivial matter-of-fact, some prosaic date or half-buried landmark, will also encounter this little secret of ours, as I may call it,—will decipher an old faint note to this effect, overlaid with the memoranda of intervening years. Of course she will. Sentiment aside, she is a woman of an excellent memory. Whether she forgives or not I know not; but she certainly doesn't forget. Doubtless, virtue is its own reward;

but there is a double satisfaction in being polite to a person on whom it *tells*. Another reason for my pleasant relations with the Captain is, that I afford him a chance to rub up his rusty old cosmopolitanism, and trot out his little scraps of old-fashioned reading, some of which are very curious. It is a great treat for him to spin his threadbare yarns over again to a sympathetic listener. These warm July evenings, in the sweet-smelling garden, are just the proper setting for his amiable garrulities. An odd enough relation subsists between us on this point. Like many gentlemen of his calling, the Captain is harassed by an irresistible desire to romance, even on the least promising themes; and it is vastly amusing to observe how he will auscultate, as it were, his auditor's inmost mood, to ascertain whether it is prepared for the absorption of his insidious fibs. Sometimes they perish utterly in the transition: they are very pretty, I conceive, in the deep and briny well of the Captain's fancy; but they won't bear being transplanted into the shallow inland lakes of my land-bred apprehension. At other times, the auditor being in a dreamy, sentimental, and altogether unprincipled mood, he will drink the old man's salt-water by the bucketful and feel none the worse for it. Which is the worse, willfully to tell, or willfully to believe, a pretty little falsehood which will not hurt anyone? I suppose you can't believe willfully; you only pretend to believe. My part of the game, therefore, is certainly as bad as the Captain's. Perhaps I take kindly to his beautiful perversions of fact, because I am myself engaged in one, because I am sailing under false colors of the deepest dye. I wonder whether my friends have any suspicion of the real state of the case. How should they? I fancy, that, on the whole, I play my part pretty well. I am delighted to find it come so easy. I do not mean that I experience little difficulty in foregoing my hundred petty elegancies and luxuries,—for to these, thank Heaven, I was not so indissolubly wedded that one wholesome shock could not loosen my bonds,—but that I manage more cleverly than I expected to stifle those innumerable tacit illusions which might serve effectually to belie my character.

Sunday, July 20th.—This has been a very pleasant day for me; although in it, of course, I have done no manner of work. I had this morning a delightful *tête-à-tête* with my hostess. She had sprained her ankle, coming downstairs; and so, instead of going forth to Sunday school and to meeting, she was obliged to remain at home on the sofa. The Captain, who is of a very punctilious piety, went off alone. When I came into the parlor, as the churchbells were ringing, Miss Blunt asked me if I never went to meeting. "Never when there is anything better to do at home," said I.

"What is better than going to church?" she asked, with charming simplicity.

She was reclining on the sofa, with her foot on a pillow, and her Bible in her lap. She looked by no means afflicted at having to be absent from divine service; and, instead of answering her question, I took the liberty of telling her so.

"I *am* sorry to be absent," said she. "You know it's my only festival in the week."

"So you look upon it as a festival," said I.

"Isn't it a pleasure to meet one's acquaintance? I confess I am never deeply interested in the sermon, and I very much dislike teaching the children; but I like wearing my best bonnet, and singing in the choir, and walking part of the way home with—"

"With whom?"

"With any one who offers to walk with me."

"With Mr. Johnson, for instance," said I.

Mr. Johnson is a young lawyer in the village, who calls here once a week, and whose attentions to Miss Blunt have been remarked.

"Yes," she answered, "Mr. Johnson will do as an instance."

"How he will miss you!"

"I suppose he will. We sing off the same book. What are you laughing at? He kindly permits me to hold the book, while he stands with his hands in his pockets. Last Sunday I quite lost patience. 'Mr. Johnson,' said I, 'do hold the book! Where are your manners?' He burst out laughing in the midst of the reading. He will certainly have to hold the book to-day."

"What a 'masterful soul' he is! I suppose he will call after meeting."

"Perhaps he will. I hope so."

"I hope he won't," said I, roundly. "I am going to sit down here and talk to you, and I wish our *tête-à-tête* not to be interrupted."

"Have you anything particular to say?"

"Nothing so particular as Mr. Johnson, perhaps."

Miss Blunt has a very pretty affectation of being more matter-of-fact than she really is.

"His rights, then," said she, "are paramount to yours."

"Ah, you admit that he has rights?"

"Not at all. I simply assert that you have none."

"I beg your pardon. I have claims which I mean to enforce. I have a claim upon your undivided attention, when I pay you a morning call."

"Your claim is certainly answered. Have I been uncivil, pray?"

"Not uncivil, perhaps, but inconsiderate. You have been sighing for the company of a third person, which you can't expect me to relish."

"Why not, pray? If I, a lady, can put up with Mr. Johnson's society, why shouldn't you, one of his own sex?"

"Because he is so outrageously conceited. You, as a lady, or at any rate as a woman, like conceited men."

"Ah, yes; I have no doubt that I, as a woman, have all kinds of improper tastes. That's an old story."

"Admit, at any rate, that our friend is conceited."

"Admit it? Why, I have said so a hundred times. I have told him so."

"Indeed! It has come to that, then?"

"To what, pray?"

"To that critical point in the friendship of a lady and gentleman, when they bring against each other all kinds of delightful charges of moral obliquity. Take care, Miss Blunt! A couple of intelligent New-Englanders, of opposite sex, young, unmarried, are pretty far gone, when they begin morally to reprobate each other. So you told Mr. Johnson that he is conceited? And I suppose you added, that he was also dreadfully satirical and skeptical? What was his rejoinder? Let me see. Did he ever tell you that you were a little bit affected?"

"No: he left that for you to say, in this very ingenious manner. Thank you, sir."

"He left it for me to deny, which is a great deal prettier. Do you think the manner ingenious?"

"I think the matter, considering the day and hour, very profane, Mr. Locksley. Suppose you go away and let me read my Bible."

"Meanwhile," I asked, "what shall I do?"

"Go and read yours, if you have one."

"I haven't."

I was, nevertheless, compelled to retire, with the promise of a second audience in half an hour. Poor Miss Blunt owes it to her conscience to read a certain number of chapters. What a pure and upright soul she is! And what an edifying spectacle is much of our feminine piety! Women find a place for everything in their commodious little minds, just as they do in their wonderfully subdivided trunks, when they go on a journey. I have no doubt that this young lady stows away her religion in a corner, just as she does her Sunday bonnet,—and, when the proper moment comes, draws it forth, and reflects while she assumes it before the glass, and blows away the strictly imaginary dust: for what worldly impurity can penetrate through half a dozen layers of cambric and tissue-paper? Dear me, what a comfort it is to have a nice, fresh, holiday faith!—When I returned to the parlor, Miss Blunt was still sitting with her Bible in her lap. Somehow or other, I no longer felt in the mood for jesting. So I asked her soberly what she had been reading. Soberly she answered me. She inquired how I had spent my half-hour.

"In thinking good Sabbath thoughts," I said. "I have been walking in the garden." And then I spoke my mind. "I have been thanking Heaven that it has led me, a poor, friendless wanderer, into so peaceful an anchorage."

"Are you, then, so poor and friendless?" asked Miss Blunt, quite abruptly.

"Did you ever hear of an art-student under thirty who wasn't poor?" I answered. "Upon my word, I have yet to sell my first picture. Then, as for being friendless, there are not five people in the world who really care for me."

"*Really* care? I am afraid you look too close. And then I think five good friends is a very large number. I think myself very well off with a couple. But if you are friendless, it's probably your own fault."

"Perhaps it is," said I, sitting down in the rocking-chair; "and yet, perhaps, it isn't. Have you found me so very repulsive? Haven't you, on the contrary, found me rather sociable?"

She folded her arms, and quietly looked at me for a moment, before answering. I shouldn't wonder if I blushed a little.

"You want a compliment, Mr. Locksley; that's the long and short of it. I have not paid you a compliment since you have been here. How you must have suffered! But it's a pity you couldn't have waited awhile longer, instead of beginning to angle with that very clumsy bait. For an artist, you are very inartistic. Men never know how to wait. 'Have I found you repulsive? haven't I found you sociable?' Perhaps, after all, considering what I have in my mind, it is as well that you asked for your compliment. I have found you charming. I say it freely; and yet I say, with equal sincerity, that I fancy very few others would find you so. I can say decidedly that you are not sociable. You are entirely too particular. You are considerate of me, because you know that I know that you are so. There's the rub, you see: I know that you know that I know it. Don't interrupt me; I am going to be eloquent. I want you to understand why I don't consider you sociable. You call Mr. Johnson conceited; but, really, I don't believe he's nearly as conceited as yourself. You are too conceited to be sociable; he is not. I am an obscure, weak-minded woman,—weak-minded, you know, compared with men. I can be patronized,—yes, that's the word. Would you be equally amiable with a person as strong, as clear-sighted as yourself, with a person equally averse with yourself to being under an obligation? I think not. Of course it's delightful to charm people. Who wouldn't? There is no harm in it, as long as the charmer does not set up for a public benefactor. If I were a man, a clever man like yourself, who had seen the world, who was not to be charmed and encouraged, but to be convinced and refuted, would you be equally amiable? It will perhaps seem absurd to you, and it will certainly seem egotistical, but I consider myself sociable, for all that I have only a couple of friends,—my father and the principal of the school. That is, I mingle with women without any second thought. Not that I wish you to do so: on the contrary, if the contrary is natural to you. But I don't believe you mingle in the same way with men. You may ask me what I know about it. Of course I know nothing: I simply guess. When I have done, indeed, I mean to beg your pardon for all I have said; but until then, give me a chance. You are incapable of listening deferentially to stupid, bigoted persons. I am not, I do it every day. Ah, you have no idea what nice manners I have in the exercise of my profession! Every day I have occasion to pocket my pride and to stifle my precious sense of the ridiculous,—of which, of course, you think I haven't a bit. It is, for instance, a constant vexation to me to be poor. It makes me frequently hate rich women; it makes me despise poor ones. I don't know whether you suffer acutely from the narrowness of your own means; but if you do, I dare say you shun rich men. I don't. I like to go into rich people's houses, and to be very polite to the ladies of the house, especially if they are very well-dressed and ignorant and vulgar. All women are like me in this respect; and all men more or less like you. That is, after all, the text of my sermon. Compared with us, it has always seemed to me that you are arrant cowards,—that we alone are brave. To be sociable, you must have a great deal of pluck. You are too fine a gentleman. Go and teach school, or open a corner grocery, or sit in a law-office all day, waiting for clients: then you will be sociable. As yet, you are only agreeable. It *is* your own fault, if people don't care for you. You don't care for them. That you should be indifferent to their applause is all very well; but you don't care for their indifference. You are amiable, you are very kind, and you are also very lazy. You consider that you are working now, don't you? Many persons would not call it work."

It was now certainly my turn to fold my arms.

"And now," added my companion, as I did so, "I beg your pardon."

"This was certainly worth waiting for," said I. "I don't know what answer to make. My head swims. I don't know whether you have been attacking me or praising me. So you advise me to open a corner grocery, do you?"

"I advise you to do something that will make you a little less satirical. You had better marry, for instance."

"*Je ne demande pas mieux.* Will you have me? I can't afford it."

"Marry a rich woman."

I shook my head.

"Why not?" asked Miss Blunt. "Because people would accuse you of being mercenary? What of that? I mean to marry the first rich man who offers. Do you know that I am tired of living alone in this weary old way, teaching little girls their gamut, and turning and patching my dresses? I mean to marry the first man who offers."

"Even if he is poor?"

"Even if he is poor, ugly, and stupid."

"I am your man, then. Would you take me, if I were to offer?"

"Try and see."

"Must I get upon my knees?"

"No, you need not even do that. Am I not on mine? It

would be too fine an irony. Remain as you are, lounging back in your chair, with your thumbs in your waistcoat."

If I were writing a romance now, instead of transcribing facts, I would say that I knew not what might have happened at this juncture, had not the door opened and admitted the Captain and Mr. Johnson. The latter was in the highest spirits.

"How are you, Miss Esther? So you have been breaking your leg, eh? How are you, Mr. Locksley? I wish I were a doctor now. Which is it, right or left?"

In this simple fashion he made himself agreeable to Miss Blunt. He stopped to dinner and talked without ceasing. Whether our hostess had talked herself out in her very animated address to myself an hour before, or whether she preferred to oppose no obstacle to Mr. Johnson's fluency, or whether she was indifferent to him, I know not; but she held her tongue with that easy grace, that charming tacit intimation of "We could, and we would," of which she is so perfect a mistress. This very interesting woman has a number of pretty traits in common with her town-bred sisters; only, whereas in these they are laboriously acquired, in her they are severely natural. I am sure, that, if I were to plant her in Madison Square tomorrow, she would, after one quick, all-compassing glance, assume the *nil admirari* in a manner to drive the greatest lady of them all to despair. Johnson is a man of excellent intentions, but no taste. Two or three times I looked at Miss Blunt to see what impression his sallies were making upon her. They seemed to produce none whatever. But I know better, *moi.* Not one of them escaped her.

But I suppose she said to herself that her impressions on this point were no business of mine. Perhaps she was right. It is a disagreeable word to use of a woman you admire; but I can't help fancying that she has been a little *soured.* By what? Who shall say? By some old love affair, perhaps.

July 24th.—This evening the Captain and I took a half-hour's turn about the harbor. I asked him frankly, as a friend, whether Johnson wants to marry his daughter.

"I guess he does," said the old man; "and yet I hope he don't. You know what he is: he's smart, promising, and already sufficiently well off. But somehow he isn't for a man what my Esther is for a woman."

"That he isn't!" said I; "and honestly, Captain Blunt, I don't know who is—"

"Unless it's yourself," said the Captain.

"Thank you. I know a great many ways in which Mr. Johnson is more worthy of her than I."

"And I know one in which you are more worthy of her than he,—that is, in being what we used to call a gentleman."

"Miss Esther made him sufficiently welcome in her quiet way, on Sunday," I rejoined.

"Oh, she respects him," said Blunt. "As she's situated, she might marry him on that. You see, she's weary of hearing little girls drum on the piano. With her ear for music," added the Captain, "I wonder she has borne it so long."

"She is certainly meant for better things," said I.

"Well," answered the Captain, who has an honest habit

of deprecating your agreement, when it occurs to him that he has obtained it for sentiments which fall somewhat short of the stoical,—"well," said he, with a very dry expression of mouth, "she's born to do her duty. We are all of us born for that."

"Sometimes our duty is rather dreary," said I.

"So it be; but what's the help for it? I don't want to die without seeing my daughter provided for. What she makes by teaching is a pretty slim subsistence. There was a time when I thought she was going to be fixed for life, but it all blew over. There was a young fellow here from down Boston way, who came about as near to it as you can come, when you actually don't. He and Esther were excellent friends. One day Esther came up to me, and looked me in the face, and told me she was engaged.

"'Who to?' says I, though, of course, I knew, and Esther told me as much. 'When do you expect to marry?' I asked.

"'When John grows rich enough,' says she.

"'When will that be?'

"'It may not be for years,' said poor Esther.

"A whole year passed, and, as far as I could see, the young man came no nearer to his fortune. He was forever running to and fro between this place and Boston. I asked no questions, because I knew that my poor girl wished it so. But at last, one day, I began to think it was time to take an observation, and see whereabouts we stood.

"'Has John made his fortune yet?' I asked.

"'I don't know, father,' said Esther.

"'When are you to be married?'

"'Never!' said my poor little girl, and burst into tears. 'Please ask me no questions,' said she. 'Our engagement is over. Ask me no questions.'

"'Tell me one thing,' said I: 'where is that d—d scoundrel who has broken my daughter's heart?'

"You should have seen the look she gave me.

"'Broken my heart, sir? You are very much mistaken. I don't know who you mean.'

"'I mean John Banister,' said I. That was his name.

"'I believe Mr. Banister is in China,' says Esther, as grand as the Queen of Sheba. And there was an end of it. I never learnt the ins and outs of it. I have been told that Banister is accumulating money very fast in the China trade."

August 7th.—I have made no entry for more than a fortnight. They tell me I have been very ill; and I find no difficulty in believing them. I suppose I took cold, sitting out so late, sketching. At all events, I have had a mild intermittent fever. I have slept so much, however, that the time has seemed rather short. I have been tenderly nursed by this kind old gentleman, his daughter, and his maid-servant. God bless them, one and all! I say his daughter, because old Dorothy informs me that for half an hour one morning, at dawn, after a night during which I had been very feeble, Miss Blunt relieved guard at my bedside, while I lay wrapt in brutal slumber. It is very jolly to see sky and ocean once again. I have got myself into my easy-chair by the open window, with my shutters closed and the lattice open; and here I sit with my book on my knee, scratching away feebly enough. Now and then I peep from my cool, dark sick-chamber out into the world of light. High noon at midsummer! What a spectacle! There are no clouds in the sky, no waves on the ocean. The sun has it all to himself. To look long at the garden makes the eyes water. And we—"Hobbs, Nobbs, Stokes, and Nokes"—propose to paint that kingdom of light. *Allons, donc!*

The loveliest of women has just tapped, and come in with a plate of early peaches. The peaches are of a gorgeous color and plumpness; but Miss Blunt looks pale and thin. The hot weather doesn't agree with her. She is overworked. Confound it! Of course I thanked her warmly for her attentions during my illness. She disclaims all gratitude, and refers me to her father and Mrs. Dorothy.

"I allude more especially," said I, "to that little hour at the end of a weary night, when you stole in like a kind of moral Aurora, and drove away the shadows from my brain. That morning, you know, I began to get better."

"It was, indeed, a very little hour," said Miss Blunt. "It was about ten minutes." And then she began to scold me for presuming to touch a pen during my convalescence. She laughs at me, indeed, for keeping a diary at all. "Of all things," cried she, "a sentimental man is the most despicable."

I confess I was somewhat nettled. The thrust seemed gratuitous.

"Of all things," I answered, "a woman without sentiment is the most unlovely."

"Sentiment and loveliness are all very well, when you have time for them," said Miss Blunt. "I haven't. I'm not rich enough. Good morning."

Speaking of another woman, I would say that she flounced out of the room. But such was the gait of Juno, when she moved stiffly over the grass from where Paris stood with Venus holding the apple, gathering up her divine vestment, and leaving the others to guess at her face—

Juno has just come back to say that she forgot what she came for half an hour ago. What will I be pleased to like for dinner?

"I have just been writing in my diary that you flounced out of the room," said I.

"Have you, indeed? Now you can write that I have bounced in. There's a nice cold chicken downstairs," etc., etc.

August 14th.—This afternoon I sent for a light wagon, and treated Miss Blunt to a drive. We went successively over the three beaches. What a time we had, coming home! I shall never forget that hard trot over Weston's Beach. The tide was very low; and we had the whole glittering, weltering strand to ourselves. There was a heavy blow yesterday, which had not yet subsided; and the waves had been lashed into a magnificent fury. Trot, trot, trot, trot, we trundled over the hard sand. The sound of the horse's hoofs rang out sharp against the monotone of the thunderous surf, as we drew nearer and nearer to the long line of the cliffs. At our left, almost from the lofty zenith of the pale evening sky to the high western horizon of the tumultuous dark-green sea, was suspended, so to speak, one of those gorgeous vertical sunsets that Turner loved so well. It was a splendid confusion of purple and green and gold,—the clouds flying and flowing in the wind like the folds of a mighty banner borne by some triumphal fleet whose prows were not visible above the long chain of mountainous waves. As we reached the point where the cliffs plunge down upon the beach, I pulled up, and we remained for some moments looking out along the low, brown, obstinate barrier at whose feet the impetuous waters were rolling themselves into powder.

August 17th.—This evening, as I lighted my bedroom candle, I saw that the Captain had something to say to me. So I waited below until the old man and his daughter had performed their usual picturesque embrace, and the latter had given me that hand-shake and that smile which I never failed to exact.

"Johnson has got his discharge," said the old man, when he had heard his daughter's door close upstairs.

"What do you mean?"

He pointed with his thumb to the room above, where we heard, through the thin partition, the movement of Miss Blunt's light step.

"You mean that he has proposed to Miss Esther?"

The Captain nodded.

"And has been refused?"

"Flat."

"Poor fellow!" said I, very honestly. "Did he tell you himself?"

"Yes, with tears in his eyes. He wanted me to speak for him. I told him it was no use. Then he began to say hard things of my poor girl."

"What kind of things?"

"A pack of falsehoods. He says she has no heart. She has promised always to regard him as a friend: it's more than I will, hang him!"

"Poor fellow!" said I; and now, as I write, I can only repeat, considering what a hope was here broken, Poor fellow!

August 23d.—I have been lounging about all day, thinking of it, dreaming of it, spooning over it, as they say. This is a decided waste of time. I think, accordingly, the best thing for me to do is, to sit down and lay the ghost by writing out my story.

On Thursday evening Miss Blunt happened to intimate that she had a holiday on the morrow, it being the birthday of the lady in whose establishment she teaches.

"There is to be a tea-party at four o'clock in the afternoon for the resident pupils and teachers," said Miss Esther. "Tea at four! what do you think of that? And then there is to be a speech-making by the smartest young lady. As my services are not required, I propose to be absent. Suppose, father, you take us out in your boat. Will you come, Mr. Locksley? We shall have a nice little picnic. Let us go over to old Fort Pudding, across the bay. We will take our dinner with us, and send Dorothy to spend the day with her sister, and put the house-key in our pocket, and not come home till we please."

I warmly espoused the project, and it was accordingly carried into execution the next morning, when, at about ten o'clock, we pushed off from our little wharf at the garden-foot. It was a perfect summer's day: I can say no more for it. We made a quiet run over to the point of our destination. I shall never forget the wondrous stillness which brooded over earth and water, as we weighed anchor in the lee of my old friend,—or old enemy,—the ruined fort. The deep, translucent water reposed at the base of the warm sunlit cliff like a great basin of glass, which I half expected to hear shiver and crack as our keel ploughed through it. And how color and sound stood out in the transparent air! How audibly the little ripples on the beach whispered to the open sky! How our irreverent voices seemed to jar upon the privacy of the little cove! The mossy rocks doubled themselves without a flaw in the clear, dark water. The gleaming white beach lay fringed with its deep deposits of odorous sea-weed, gleaming black. The steep, straggling sides of the cliffs raised aloft their rugged angles against the burning blue of the sky. I remember, when Miss Blunt stepped ashore and stood upon the beach, relieved against the heavy shadow of a recess in the cliff, while her father and I busied ourselves with gathering up our baskets and fastening the anchor—I remember, I say, what a figure she made. There is a certain purity in this Cragthorpe air which I have never seen approached,—a lightness, a brilliancy, a *crudity*, which allows perfect liberty of self-assertion to each individual object in the landscape. The prospect is ever more or less like a picture which lacks its final process, its reduction to unity. Miss Blunt's figure, as she stood there on the beach, was almost *criarde;* but how lovely it was! Her light muslin dress, gathered up over her short white skirt, her little black mantilla, the blue veil which she had knotted about her neck, the crimson shawl which she had thrown over her arm, the little silken dome which she poised over her head in one gloved hand, while the other retained her crisp draperies, and which cast down upon her face a sharp circle of shade, out of which her cheerful eyes shone darkly and her happy mouth smiled whitely,—these are some of the hastily noted points of the picture.

"Young woman," I cried out, over the water, "I do wish you might know how pretty you look!"

"How do you know I don't?" she answered. "I should think I might. You don't look so badly, yourself. But it's not I; it's the accessories."

"Hang it! I am going to become profane," I called out again.

"Swear ahead," said the Captain.

"I am going to say you are devilish pretty."

"Dear me! is that all?" cried Miss Blunt, with a little light laugh, which must have made the tutelar sirens of the cove ready to die with jealousy down in their submarine bowers.

By the time the Captain and I had landed our effects, our companion had tripped lightly up the forehead of the cliff—in one place it is very retreating—and disappeared over its crown. She soon reappeared with an intensely white handkerchief added to her other provocations, which she waved to us, as we trudged upward, carrying our baskets. When we stopped to take breath on the summit, and wipe our foreheads, we, of course, rebuked her who was roaming about idly with her parasol and gloves.

"Do you think I am going to take any trouble or do any

work?" cried Miss Esther, in the greatest good-humor. "Is not this my holiday? I am not going to raise a finger, nor soil these beautiful gloves, for which I paid a dollar at Mr. Dawson's in Cragthorpe. After you have found a shady place for your provisions, I would like you to look for a spring. I am very thirsty."

"Find the spring yourself, Miss," said her father. "Mr. Locksley and I have a spring in this basket. Take a pull, sir."

And the Captain drew forth a stout black bottle.

"Give me a cup, and I will look for some water," said Miss Blunt. "Only I'm so afraid of the snakes! If you hear a scream, you may know it's a snake."

"Screaming snakes!" said I; "that's a new species."

What nonsense it all sounds like now! As we looked about us, shade seemed scarce, as it generally is, in this region. But Miss Blunt, like the very adroit and practical young person she is, for all that she would have me believe the contrary, soon discovered a capital cool spring in the shelter of a pleasant little dell, beneath a clump of firs. Hither, as one of the young gentlemen who imitate Tennyson would say, we brought our basket, Blunt and I; while Esther dipped the cup, and held it dripping to our thirsty lips, and laid the cloth, and on the grass disposed the platters round. I should have to be a poet, indeed, to describe half the happiness and the silly poetry and purity and beauty of this bright long summer's day. We ate, drank, and talked; we ate occasionally with our ringers, we drank out of the necks of our bottles, and we talked with our mouths full, as befits (and excuses) those who talk wild nonsense. We told stories without the least point. Blunt and I made atrocious puns. I believe, indeed, that Miss Blunt herself made one little pun-kin, as I called it. If there had been any superfluous representative of humanity present, to register the fact, I should say that we made fools of ourselves. But as there was no fool on hand, I need say nothing about it. I am conscious myself of having said several witty things, which Miss Blunt understood: *in vino veritas*. The dear old Captain twanged the long bow indefatigably. The bright high sun lingered above us the livelong day, and drowned the prospect with light and warmth. One of these days I mean to paint a picture which in future ages, when my dear native land shall boast a national school of art, will hang in the *Salon Carré* of the great central museum, (located, let us say, in Chicago,) and remind folks—or rather make them forget—Giorgione, Bordone, and Veronese: A Rural Festival; three persons feasting under some trees; scene, nowhere in particular; time and hour, problematical. Female figure, a big *brune;* young man reclining on his elbow; old man drinking. An empty sky, with no end of expression. The whole stupendous in color, drawing, feeling. Artist uncertain; supposed to be Robinson, 1900. That's about the program.

After dinner the Captain began to look out across the bay, and, noticing the uprising of a little breeze, expressed a wish to cruise about for an hour or two. He proposed to us to walk along the shore to a point a couple of miles northward, and there meet the boat. His daughter having agreed to this proposition, he set off with the lightened pannier, and in less than half an hour we saw him standing out from shore. Miss

Blunt and I did not begin our walk for a long, long time. We sat and talked beneath the trees. At our feet, a wide cleft in the hills—almost a glen—stretched down to the silent beach. Beyond lay the familiar ocean-line. But, as many philosophers have observed, there is an end to all things. At last we got up. Miss Blunt said, that, as the air was freshening, she believed she would put on her shawl. I helped her to fold it into the proper shape, and then I placed it on her shoulders, her crimson shawl over her black silk sack. And then she tied her veil once more about her neck, and gave me her hat to hold, while she effected a partial redistribution of her hair-pins. By way of being humorous, I placed her hat on my own head; at which she was kind enough to smile, as with downcast face and uplifted elbows she fumbled among her braids. And then she shook out the creases of her dress, and drew on her gloves; and finally she said, "Well!"—that inevitable tribute to time and morality which follows upon even the mildest form of dissipation. Very slowly it was that we wandered down the little glen. Slowly, too, we followed the course of the narrow and sinuous beach, as it keeps to the foot of the low cliffs. We encountered no sign of human interest. Our conversation I need hardly repeat. I think I may trust it to the keeping of my memory; I think I shall be likely to remember it. It was all very sober and sensible,—such talk as it is both easy and pleasant to remember; it was even prosaic,—or, at least, if there was a vein of poetry in it, I should have defied a listener to put his finger on it. There was no exaltation of feeling or utterance on either side; on one side, indeed, there was very little utterance. Am I wrong in conjecturing, however, that there was considerable feeling of a certain quiet kind? Miss Blunt maintained a rich, golden silence. I, on the other hand, was very voluble. What a sweet, womanly listener she is!

September 1st.—I have been working steadily for a week. This is the first day of autumn. Read aloud to Miss Blunt a little Wordsworth.

September 10th. Midnight.—Worked without interruption,—until yesterday, inclusive, that is. But with the day now closing—or opening—begins a new era. My poor vapid old diary, at last you shall hold a *fact.*

For three days past we have been having damp, chilly weather. Dusk has fallen early. This evening, after tea, the Captain went into town,—on business, as he said: I believe, to attend some Poorhouse or Hospital Board. Esther and I went into the parlor. The room seemed cold. She brought in the lamp from the dining-room, and proposed we should have a little fire. I went into the kitchen, procured an armful of wood, and while she drew the curtains and wheeled up the table, I kindled a lively, crackling blaze. A fortnight ago she would not have allowed me to do this without a protest. She would not have offered to do it herself,—not she!—but she would have said that I was not here to serve, but to be served, and would have pretended to call Dorothy. Of course I should have had my own way. But we have changed all that. Esther went to her piano, and I sat down to a book. I read not a word. I sat looking at my mistress, and thinking with a very uneasy heart. For the first time in our friendship, she had put on a dark, warm dress: I think it was of the material called alpaca. The first time I saw her she wore a white dress with a purple neck-ribbon; now she wore a black dress with the same ribbon. That is, I remember wondering, as I sat there eyeing her, whether it was the same ribbon, or merely another like it. My heart was in my throat; and yet I thought of a number of trivialities of the same kind. At last I spoke.

"Miss Blunt," I said, "do you remember the first evening I passed beneath your roof, last June?"

"Perfectly," she replied, without stopping.

"You played this same piece."

"Yes; I played it very badly, too. I only half knew it. But it is a showy piece, and I wished to produce an effect. I didn't know then how indifferent you are to music."

"I paid no particular attention to the piece. I was intent upon the performer."

"So the performer supposed."

"What reason had you to suppose so?"

"I'm sure I don't know. Did you ever know a woman to be able to give a reason, when she has guessed aright?"

"I think they generally contrive to make up a reason, afterwards. Come, what was yours?"

"Well, you *stared* so hard."

"Fie! I don't believe it. That's unkind."

"You said you wished me to invent a reason. If I really had one, I don't remember it."

"You told me you remembered the occasion in question perfectly."

"I meant the circumstances. I remember what we had for tea; I remember what dress I wore. But I don't remember my feelings. They were naturally not very memorable."

"What did you say, when your father proposed my coming?"

"I asked how much you would be willing to pay."

"And then?"

"And then, if you looked 'respectable.'"

"And then?"

"That was all. I told father that he could do as he pleased."

She continued to play. Leaning back in my chair, I continued to look at her. There was a considerable pause.

"Miss Esther," said I, at last.

"Yes."

"Excuse me for interrupting you so often. But,"—and I got up and went to the piano,—"but I thank Heaven that it has brought you and me together."

She looked up at me and bowed her head with a little smile, as her hands still wandered over the keys.

"Heaven has certainly been very good to us," said she.

"How much longer are you going to play?" I asked.

"I'm sure I don't know. As long as you like."

"If you want to do as I like, you will stop immediately."

She let her hands rest on the keys a moment, and gave me a rapid, questioning look. Whether she found a sufficient answer in my face I know not; but she slowly rose, and, with a very pretty affectation of obedience, began to close the instrument. I helped her to do so.

"Perhaps you would like to be quite alone," she said. "I suppose your own room is too cold."

"Yes," I answered, "you've hit it exactly. I wish to be alone. I wish to monopolize this cheerful blaze. Hadn't you better go into the kitchen and sit with the cook? It takes you women to make such cruel speeches."

"When we women are cruel, Mr. Locksley, it is without knowing it. We are not willfully so. When we learn that we have been unkind, we very humbly ask pardon, without even knowing what our crime has been." And she made me a very low curtsy.

"I will tell you what your crime has been," said I. "Come and sit by the fire. It's rather a long story."

"A long story? Then let me get my work."

"Confound your work! Excuse me, but I mean it. I want you to listen to me. Believe me, you will need all your thoughts."

She looked at me steadily a moment, and I returned her glance. During that moment I was reflecting whether I might silently emphasize my request by laying a lover's hand upon her shoulder. I decided that I might not. She walked over and quietly seated herself in a low chair by the fire. Here she patiently folded her arms. I sat down before her.

"With you, Miss Blunt," said I, "one must be very explicit. You are not in the habit of taking things for granted. You have a great deal of imagination, but you rarely exercise it on the behalf of other people." I stopped a moment.

"Is that my crime?" asked my companion.

"It's not so much a crime as a vice," said I; "and perhaps not so much a vice as a virtue. Your crime is, that you are so stone-cold to a poor devil who loves you."

She burst into a rather shrill laugh. I wonder whether she thought I meant Johnson.

"Who are you speaking for, Mr. Locksley?" she asked.

"Are there so many? For myself."

"Honestly?"

"Honestly doesn't begin to express it."

"What is that French phrase that you are forever using? I think I may say, '*Allons, donc!*'"

"Let us speak plain English, Miss Blunt."

"'Stone-cold' is certainly very plain English. I don't see the relative importance of the two branches of your proposition. Which is the principal, and which the subordinate clause,—that I am stone-cold, as you call it, or that you love me, as you call it?"

"As I call it? What would you have me call it? For God's sake, Miss Blunt, be serious, or I shall call it something else. Yes, I love you. Don't you believe it?"

"I am open to conviction."

"Thank God!" said I.

And I attempted to take her hand.

"No, no, Mr. Locksley," said she,— "not just yet; if you please."

"Action speaks louder than words," said I.

"There is no need of speaking loud. I hear you perfectly."

"I certainly sha'n't whisper," said I; "although it is the custom, I believe, for lovers to do so. Will you be my wife?"

"I sha'n't whisper, either, Mr. Locksley. Yes, I will."

And now she put out her hand.—That's my fact.

September 12th.—We are to be married within three weeks.

September 19th.—I have been in New York a week, transacting business. I got back yesterday. I find every one here talking about our engagement. Esther tells me that it was talked about a month ago, and that there is a very general feeling of disappointment that I am not rich.

"Really, if you don't mind it," said I, "I don't see why others should."

"I don't know whether you are rich or not," says Esther; "but I know that I am."

"Indeed! I was not aware that you had a private fortune," etc., etc.

This little farce is repeated in some shape every day. I am very idle. I smoke a great deal, and lounge about all day, with my hands in my pockets. I am free from that ineffable weariness of ceaseless *giving* which I experienced six months ago. I was shorn of my hereditary trinkets at that period; and I have resolved that *this* engagement, at all events, shall have no connection with the shops. I was balked of my poetry once; I sha'n't be a second time. I don't think there is much danger of this. Esther deals it out with full hands. She takes a very pretty interest in her simple outfit,—showing me triumphantly certain of her purchases, and making a great mystery about others, which she is pleased to denominate table-cloths and napkins. Last evening I found her sewing buttons on a tablecloth. I had heard a great deal of a certain gray silk dress; and this morning, accordingly, she marched up to me, arrayed in this garment. It is trimmed with velvet, and hath flounces, a train, and all the modern improvements generally.

"There is only one objection to it," said Esther, parading before the glass in my painting-room: "I am afraid it is above our station."

"By Jove! I'll paint your portrait in it," said I, "and make our fortune. All the other men who have handsome wives will bring them to be painted."

"You mean all the women who have handsome dresses," said Esther, with great humility.

Our wedding is fixed for next Thursday. I tell Esther that it will be as little of a wedding, and as much of a marriage, as possible. Her father and her good friend the schoolmistress alone are to be present.—My secret oppresses me considerably; but I have resolved to keep it for the honeymoon, when it may take care of itself. I am harassed with a dismal apprehension, that, if Esther were to discover it now, the whole thing would be *à refaire.* I have taken rooms at a romantic little watering-place called Clifton, ten miles off. The hotel is already quite free of city-people, and we shall be almost alone.

September 28th.—We have been here two days. The little transaction in the church went off smoothly. I am truly sorry for the Captain. We drove directly over here, and reached the place at dusk. It was a raw, black day. We have a couple of good rooms, close to the savage sea. I am nevertheless afraid I have made a mistake. It would perhaps have been wiser to go inland. These things are not immaterial: we make our own heaven, but we scarcely make our own earth. I am writing at a little table by the window, looking out on the rocks, the gathering dusk, and the rising fog. My wife has wandered down to the rocky platform in front of the house. I can see her from here, bareheaded, in that old crimson shawl, talking to one of the landlord's little boys. She has just given the little fellow a kiss, bless her heart! I remember her telling me once that she was very fond of little boys; and, indeed, I have noticed that they are seldom too dirty for her to take on her knee. I have been reading over these pages for the first time in—I don't know when. They are filled with *her*,—even more in thought than in word. I believe I will show them to her, when she comes in. I will give her the book to read, and sit by her, watching her face,—watching the great secret dawn upon her.

Later.—Somehow or other, I can write this quietly enough; but I hardly think I shall ever write any more. When Esther came in, I handed her this book.

"I want you to read it," said I.

She turned very pale, and laid it on the table, shaking her head.

"I know it," she said.

"What do you know?"

"That you have a hundred thousand a year. But, believe me, Mr. Locksley, I am none the worse for the knowledge. You intimated in one place in your book that I am born for wealth and splendor. I believe I am. You pretend to hate your money; but you would not have had me without it. If you really love me,—and I think you do,—you will not let this make any difference. I am not such a fool as to attempt to talk here about my sensations. But I remember what I said."

"What do you expect me to do?" I asked. "Shall I call you some horrible name and cast you off?"

"I expect you to show the same courage that I am showing. I never said I loved you. I never deceived you in that. I said I would be your wife. So I will, faithfully. I haven't so much heart as you think; and yet, too, I have a great deal more. I am incapable of more than one deception.—Mercy! didn't you see it? didn't you know it? see that I saw it? know that I knew it? It was diamond cut diamond. You deceived me; I deceived you. Now that your deception ceases, mine ceases. *Now* we are free, with our hundred thousand a year! Excuse me, but it sometimes comes across me! Now we can be good and honest and true. It was all a make-believe virtue before."

"So you read that thing?" I asked: actually—strange as it may seem—for something to say.

"Yes, while you were ill. It was lying with your pen in it, on the table. I read it because I suspected. Otherwise I shouldn't have done so."

"It was the act of a false woman," said I.

"A false woman? No,—simply of a woman. I am a woman, sir." And she began to smile. "Come, *you* be a man!"

A Wagner Matinee

Willa Cather

First published in The Troll Garden *by McClure, Phillips & Company, 1905.*

I received one morning a letter, written in pale ink on glassy, blue-lined notepaper, and bearing the postmark of a little Nebraska village. This communication, worn and rubbed, looking as though it had been carried for some days in a coat pocket that was none too clean, was from my uncle Howard and informed me that his wife had been left a small legacy by a bachelor relative who had recently died, and that it would be necessary for her to go to Boston to attend to the settling of the estate. He requested me to meet her at the station and render her whatever services might be necessary. On examining the date indicated as that of her arrival, I found it no later than tomorrow. He had characteristically delayed writing until, had I been away from home for a day, I must have missed the good woman altogether.

The name of my Aunt Georgiana called up not alone her own figure, at once pathetic and grotesque, but opened before my feet a gulf of recollection so wide and deep that, as the letter dropped from my hand, I felt suddenly a stranger to all the present conditions of my existence, wholly ill at ease and out of place amid the familiar surroundings of my study. I became, in short, the gangling farm boy my aunt had known, scourged with chilblains and bashfulness, my hands cracked and sore from the corn husking. I felt the knuckles of my thumb tentatively, as though they were raw again. I sat again before her parlor organ, fumbling the scales with my stiff, red hands, while she, beside me, made canvas mittens for the huskers.

The next morning, after preparing my landlady somewhat, I set out for the station. When the train arrived I had some difficulty in finding my aunt. She was the last of the passengers to alight, and it was not until I got her into the carriage that she seemed really to recognize me. She had come all the way in a day coach; her linen duster had become black with soot and her black bonnet gray with dust during the journey. When we arrived at my boardinghouse the landlady put her to bed at once and I did not see her again until the next morning.

Whatever shock Mrs. Springer experienced at my aunt's appearance, she considerately concealed. As for myself, I saw my aunt's misshapen figure with that feeling of awe and respect with which we behold explorers who have left their ears and fingers north of Franz Josef Land, or their health somewhere along the Upper Congo. My Aunt Georgiana had been a music teacher at the Boston Conservatory, somewhere back in the latter sixties. One summer, while visiting in the little village among the Green Mountains where her ancestors had dwelt for generations, she had kindled the callow fancy of the most idle and shiftless of all the village lads, and had conceived for this Howard Carpenter one of those extravagant passions which a handsome country boy of twenty-one sometimes inspires in an angular, spectacled woman of thirty. When she returned to her duties in Boston, Howard followed her, and the upshot of this inexplicable infatuation was that she eloped with him, eluding the reproaches of her family and the criticisms of her friends by going with him to the Nebraska frontier. Carpenter, who, of course, had no money, had taken a homestead in Red Willow County, fifty miles from the railroad. There they had measured off their quarter section themselves by driving across the prairie in a wagon, to the wheel of which they had tied a red cotton handkerchief, and counting off its revolutions. They built a dugout in the red hillside, one of those cave dwellings whose inmates so often reverted to primitive conditions. Their water they got from the lagoons where the buffalo drank, and their slender stock of provisions was always at the mercy of bands of roving Indians. For thirty years my aunt had not been further than fifty miles from the homestead.

But Mrs. Springer knew nothing of all this, and must have been considerably shocked at what was left of my kinswoman. Beneath the soiled linen duster which, on her arrival, was the most conspicuous feature of her costume, she wore a black stuff dress, whose ornamentation showed that she had surrendered herself unquestioningly into the hands of a country dressmaker. My poor aunt's figure, however, would have presented astonishing difficulties to any dressmaker.

Originally stooped, her shoulders were now almost bent together over her sunken chest. She wore no stays, and her gown, which trailed unevenly behind, rose in a sort of peak over her abdomen. She wore ill-fitting false teeth, and her skin was as yellow as a Mongolian's from constant exposure to a pitiless wind and to the alkaline water which hardens the most transparent cuticle into a sort of flexible leather.

I owed to this woman most of the good that ever came my way in my boyhood, and had a reverential affection for her. During the years when I was riding herd for my uncle, my aunt, after cooking the three meals—the first of which was ready at six o'clock in the morning—and putting the six children to bed, would often stand until midnight at her ironing board, with me at the kitchen table beside her, hearing me recite Latin declensions and conjugations, gently shaking me when my drowsy head sank down over a page of irregular verbs. It was to her, at her ironing or mending, that I read my first Shakespeare, and her old textbook on mythology was the first that ever came into my empty hands. She taught me my scales and exercises, too—on the little parlor organ, which her husband had bought her after fifteen years, during which she had not so much as seen any instrument, but an accordion that belonged to one of the Norwegian farmhands. She would sit beside me by the hour, darning and counting while I struggled with the "Joyous Farmer," but she seldom talked to me about music, and I understood why. She was a pious woman; she had the consolations of religion and, to her at least, her martyrdom was not wholly sordid. Once when I had been doggedly beating out some easy passages

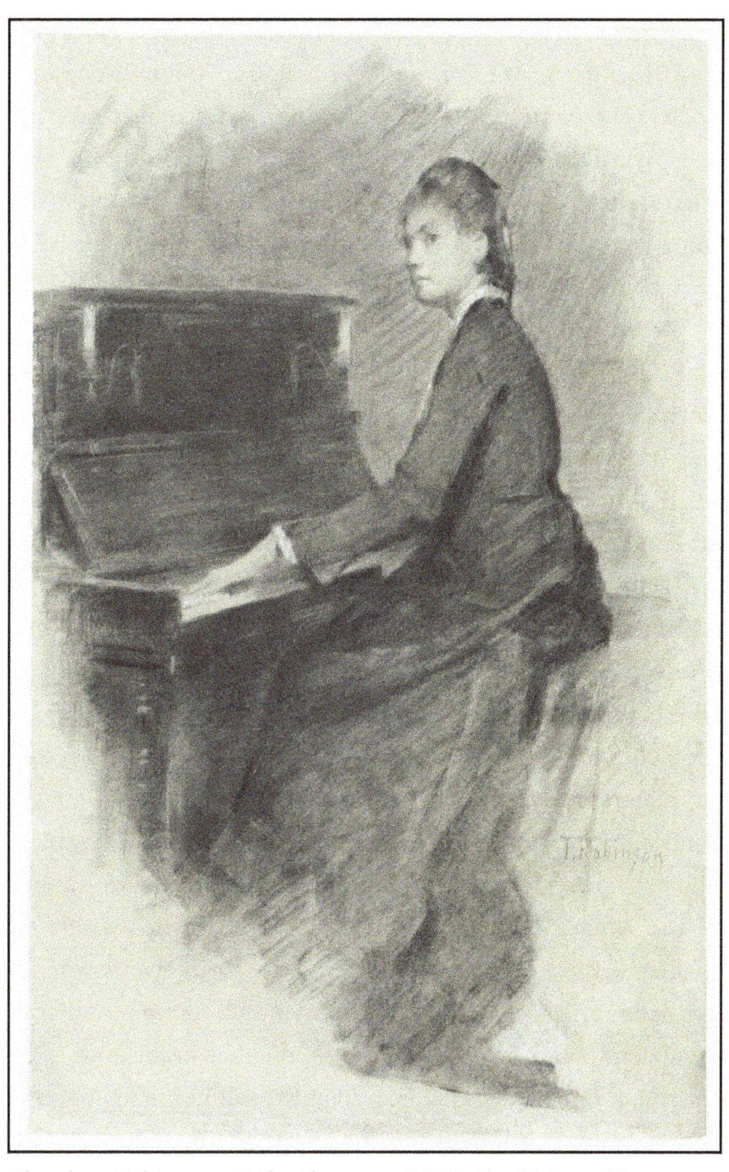

Theodore Robinson, *At the Piano*, ca. 1887, The Metropolitan Museum of Art, New York, Sheila and Richard J. Schwartz Fund, 1986

from an old score of *Euryanthe* I had found among her music books, she came up to me and, putting her hands over my eyes, gently drew my head back upon her shoulder, saying tremulously, "Don't love it so well, Clark, or it may be taken from you. Oh! dear boy, pray that whatever your sacrifice may be, it be not that."

When my aunt appeared on the morning after her arrival, she was still in a semi-somnambulant state. She seemed not to realize that she was in the city where she had spent her youth, the place longed for hungrily half a lifetime. She had been so wretchedly train-sick throughout the journey that she had no recollection of anything but her discomfort, and, to all intents and purposes, there were but a few hours of nightmare between the farm in Red Willow County and my study on Newbury Street. I had planned a little pleasure for her that afternoon, to repay her for some of the glorious moments she had given me when we used to milk together in the straw-thatched cowshed and she, because I was more than usually tired, or because her husband had spoken sharply to me, would tell me of the splendid performance of the *Huguenots* she had seen in Paris, in her youth. At two o'clock the Symphony Orchestra was to give a Wagner program, and I intended to take my aunt; though, as I conversed with her I grew doubtful about her enjoyment of it. Indeed, for her own sake, I could only wish her taste for such things quite dead, and the long struggle mercifully ended at last. I suggested our visiting the Conservatory and the Common before lunch, but she seemed altogether too timid to wish to venture out. She questioned me absently about various changes in the city, but she was chiefly concerned that she had forgotten to leave instructions about feeding half-skimmed milk to a certain weakling calf, "old Maggie's calf, you know, Clark," she explained, evidently having forgotten how long I had been away. She was further troubled because she had neglected to tell her daughter about the freshly opened kit of mackerel in the cellar, which would spoil if it were not used directly.

I asked her whether she had ever heard any of the Wagnerian operas, and found that she had not, though she was perfectly familiar with their respective situations, and had once possessed the piano score of *The Flying Dutchman*. I began to think it would have been best to get her back to Red Willow County without waking her, and regretted having suggested the concert.

From the time we entered the concert hall, however, she was a trifle less passive and inert, and for the first time seemed to perceive her surroundings. I had felt some trepidation lest she might become aware of the absurdities of her attire, or might experience some painful embarrassment at stepping suddenly into the world to which she had been dead for a quarter of a century. But, again, I found how superficially I had judged her. She sat looking about her with eyes as impersonal, almost as stony, as those with which the granite Rameses in a museum watches the froth and fret that ebbs and flows about his pedestal—separated from it by the lonely stretch of centuries. I have seen this same aloofness in old miners who drift into the Brown Hotel at Denver, their pockets full of bullion, their linen soiled, their haggard faces unshaven; standing in the thronged corridors as solitary as though they were still in a frozen camp on the Yukon, conscious that certain experiences have isolated them from their fellows by a gulf no haberdasher could bridge.

We sat at the extreme left of the first balcony, facing the arch of our own and the balcony above us, veritable hanging gardens, brilliant as tulip beds. The matinée audience was made up chiefly of women. One lost the contour of faces and figures, indeed any effect of line whatever, and there was only the color of bodices past counting the shimmer of fabrics soft and firm, silky and sheer; red, mauve, pink, blue, lilac, purple, ecru, rose, yellow, cream, and white, all the colors that an impressionist finds in a sunlit landscape, with here and there the dead shadow of a frock coat. My Aunt Georgiana regarded them as though they had been so many daubs of tube-paint on a palette.

When the musicians came out and took their places, she gave a little stir of anticipation, and looked with quickening interest down over the rail at that invariable grouping, perhaps the first wholly familiar thing that had greeted her eye since she had left old Maggie and her weakling calf. I could feel how all those details sank into her soul, for I had not forgotten how they had sunk into mine when I came fresh from plowing forever and forever between green aisles of corn, where, as in a treadmill, one might walk from daybreak to dusk without perceiving a shadow of change. The clean profiles of the musicians, the gloss of their linen, the dull black of their coats, the beloved shapes of the instruments, the patches of yellow light thrown by the green-shaded lamps on the smooth, varnished bellies of the cellos and the bass viols in the rear, the restless, wind-tossed forest of fiddle necks and bows—I recalled how, in the first orchestra I had ever heard, those long bow strokes seemed to draw the heart out of me, as a conjurer's stick reels out yards of paper ribbon from a hat.

The first number was the *Tannhauser* overture. When the horns drew out the first strain of the Pilgrim's chorus, my Aunt Georgiana clutched my coat sleeve. Then it was I first realized that for her this broke a silence of thirty years; the inconceivable silence of the plains. With the battle between the two motives, with the frenzy of the Venusberg theme and its ripping of strings, there came to me an overwhelming sense of the waste and wear we are so powerless to combat; and I saw again the tall, naked house on the prairie, black and grim as a wooden fortress; the black pond where I had learned to swim, its margin pitted with sun-dried cattle tracks; the rain-gullied clay banks about the naked house, the four dwarf ash seedlings where the dishcloths were always hung to dry before the kitchen door. The world there was the flat world of the ancients; to the east, a cornfield that stretched to daybreak; to the west, a corral that reached to sunset; between, the conquests of peace, dearer bought than those of war.

The overture closed, my aunt released my coat sleeve, but she said nothing. She sat staring at the orchestra through a dullness of thirty years, through the films made little by little by each of the three hundred and sixty-five days in every one of them. What, I wondered, did she get from it? She had been a good pianist in her day I knew, and her musical education had been broader than that of most music teachers of a quarter of a century ago. She had often told me of Mozart's operas and Meyerbeer's, and I could remember hearing her sing, years ago, certain melodies of Verdi's. When I had fallen ill with a fever in her house she used to sit by my cot in the evening—when the cool, night wind blew in through the faded mosquito netting tacked over the window and I lay watching a certain bright star that burned red above the cornfield—and sing "Home to our mountains, O, let us return!" in a way fit to break the heart of a Vermont boy near dead of homesickness already.

I watched her closely through the prelude to *Tristan and Isolde*, trying vainly to conjecture what that seething turmoil of strings and winds might mean to her, but she sat mutely staring at the violin bows that drove obliquely downward, like the pelting streaks of rain in a summer shower. Had this music any message for her? Had she enough left to at all comprehend this power which had kindled the world since she had left it? I was in a fever of curiosity, but Aunt Georgiana sat silent upon her peak in Darien. She preserved this utter immobility throughout the number from *The Flying Dutchman*, though her fingers worked mechanically upon her black dress, as though, of themselves, they were recalling the piano score they had once played. Poor old hands! They had been stretched and twisted into mere tentacles to hold and lift and knead with; the palms, unduly swollen, the fingers bent and knotted—on one of them a thin, worn band that had once been a wedding ring. As I pressed and gently quieted one of those groping hands, I remembered with quivering eyelids their services for me in other days.

Soon after the tenor began the "Prize Song," I heard a quick drawn breath and turned to my aunt. Her eyes were closed, but the tears were glistening on her cheeks, and I think, in a moment more, they were in my eyes as well. It never really died, then—the soul that can suffer so excruciatingly and so interminably; it withers to the outward eye only; like that strange moss which can lie on a dusty shelf half a century and yet, if placed in water, grows green again. She wept so throughout the development and elaboration of the melody.

During the intermission before the second half of the concert, I questioned my aunt and found that the "Prize Song" was not new to her. Some years before there had drifted to the farm in Red Willow County a young German, a tramp cowpuncher, who had sung the chorus at Bayreuth, when he was a boy, along with the other peasant boys and girls. Of a Sunday morning he used to sit on his gingham-sheeted bed in the hands' bedroom which opened off the kitchen, cleaning the leather of his boots and saddle, singing the "Prize Song," while my aunt went about her work in the kitchen. She had hovered about him until she had prevailed upon him to join the country church, though his sole fitness for this step, insofar as I could gather, lay in his boyish face and his possession of this divine melody. Shortly afterward he had gone to town on the Fourth of July, been drunk for several days, lost his money at a faro table, ridden a saddled Texan steer on a bet, and disappeared with a fractured collarbone. All this my aunt told me huskily, wanderingly, as though she were talking in the weak lapses of illness.

"Well, we have come to better things than the old *Trovatore* at any rate, Aunt Georgie?" I queried, with a well-meant effort at jocularity.

Her lip quivered and she hastily put her handkerchief up to her mouth. From behind it she murmured, "And you have been hearing this ever since you left me, Clark?" Her question was the gentlest and saddest of reproaches.

The second half of the program consisted of four numbers from the *Ring*, and closed with Siegfried's funeral march. My aunt wept quietly, but almost continuously, as a shallow vessel overflows in a rainstorm. From time to time her dim eyes looked up at the lights which studded the ceiling, burning softly under their dull glass globes; doubtless they were stars in truth to her. I was still perplexed as to what measure of musical comprehension was left to her, she who had heard nothing but the singing of gospel hymns at Methodist services in the square frame schoolhouse on Section Thirteen for so many years. I was wholly unable to gauge how much of it had been dissolved in soapsuds, or worked into bread, or milked into the bottom of a pail.

The deluge of sound poured on and on; I never knew what she found in the shining current of it; I never knew how far it bore her, or past what happy islands. From the trembling of her face I could well believe that before the last numbers she had been carried out where the myriad graves are, into the gray, nameless burying grounds of the sea; or into some world of death vaster yet, where, from the beginning of the world, hope has lain down with hope and dream with dream and, renouncing, slept.

The concert was over; the people filed out of the hall chattering and laughing, glad to relax and find the living level again, but my kinswoman made no effort to rise. The harpist slipped its green felt cover over his instrument; the flute players shook the water from their mouthpieces; the men of the orchestra went out one by one, leaving the stage to the chairs and music stands, empty as a winter cornfield.

I spoke to my aunt. She burst into tears and sobbed pleadingly. "I don't want to go, Clark, I don't want to go!"

I understood. For her, just outside the door of the concert hall, lay the black pond with the cattle-tracked bluffs; the tall, unpainted house, with weather-curled boards; naked as a tower, the crook-backed ash seedlings where the dishcloths hung to dry; the gaunt, molting turkeys picking up refuse about the kitchen door.

www.ingramcontent.com/pod-product-compliance
Lightning Source LLC
LaVergne TN
LVHW010610110826
845149LV00003B/848

* 9 7 8 0 9 9 9 4 0 0 6 9 2 *